millersburg

millersburg

Harry Cauley

THE PERMANENT PRESS

Sag Harbor, New York 11963

Library of Congress Cataloging-in-Publication Data

Cauley, Harry.
   Millersburg / Harry Cauley.
      p. cm.
   Novel.
   ISBN 1-57962-133-3 (alk. paper)
   I. Title.

PS3553.A943M55 2006
813'.54—dc22   2006046589

The Permanent Press
4170 Noyac Road
Sag Harbor, NY 11963

Chapter I

The summer of my seventeenth birthday Mamu announced that she was going to "get off the carousel," her metaphor for dying, before the end of September. That same summer there was a grisly double murder in Millersburg. It was a lurid affair, involving sex and mutilation and money and power and revenge which obviously overshadowed both my birthday and Mamu's plans to pass on. The murders took place at one of the sumptuous "cottages" on Miller Lake. Such a dreadful thing, to hear the locals talk, would never involve any of the permanent residents of the town, but the summer people, well, they were capable of almost anything and were always suspect. Primarily because they owned the most sought-after real estate surrounding the lake. The fact that they also brought revenue to a town that had little or no way of engendering income didn't matter. They were outsiders. And because one of the slain was "old money" and one internationally famous the crime made headlines around the world, giving the press a welcomed relief from having to write the ubiquitous stories about the impending Second World War. It was the most sensational crime in New Jersey since the kidnapping of the Lindbergh baby and sleepy little Millersburg was suddenly on the map of the globe and the Millersburgians had something they would talk about for decades to come.

That stiflingly hot summer of 1939 was indelibly stamped into my memory because the murders eventually involved my family. The drama of Mamu's passing was totally eclipsed, which infuriated her no end, so she postponed getting off the carousel for another twenty-two years when she died in 1961 at the age of ninety-two from eating poison mushrooms that she herself had gathered in the woods. Her eyesight had failed, but she refused to wear glasses and couldn't quite see what she was picking.

My grandmother, Adela Pritchard Wayland, became Mamu when my mother, a baby stumbling over her first words, tried to say "mommy" and it came out something like "Mamu." From that day on she was Mamu to everyone in the family and anyone in Millersburg who was on a first-name basis with her. My mother, Eulalie Wayland Whyte, my sister Estella, and I lived with Mamu in the enormous white clapboard house about two miles outside of Millersburg, and about a quarter of a mile off Route 13, on a dusty no-name dirt road we always called Broadway. It was lined with impressive old maples and elms and oaks which provided cool shade from May until the last leaves fell in mid-November. The house was kept in pristine con-dition, attended to as regularly as an historic landmark that might attract interested visitors. But our house had very few visitors. It was a house, in spite of its size, that accommodated and served the people who lived there and no one else. A wide, airy, roofed porch enclosed three sides almost like a protective moat, distancing the house from anything or anyone who might threaten or intrude. There were patches of stained glass in the upstairs windows, artfully arranged to break up the monotony of the whiteness. The south wall, the back of the house, had one door leading to the mud porch and even-tually the kitchen and one window in the upstairs bathroom, but otherwise it was blank, shielding the interior of the house from the summer heat.

Most of the rooms were not lived in and the drapes were kept closed so the sun wouldn't fade the carpets. We used the kitchen, baths, and bedrooms but almost never went into the two sitting rooms, across from each other on either side of the wide dark hallway, the dining room, the small study, the library or the sewing room. If anyone but Mamu was discovered in these rooms when there was no apparent reason to be there we were accused of snooping. There was never the slightest hint of dust and the furniture looked as though it had just come out of a showroom. The good china, which was only used on Christmas and, if Mamu was feeling festive, on Thanksgiving, was washed regularly along with the good silver and crystal which was also rarely used. There were summer curtains that replaced the winter window dressing in the rooms we lived in precisely on the fifteenth of May and came down on the fifteenth of September even if those days fell on a Sunday. Walls and woodwork were washed regularly whether they needed it or not and weekly, every window in the house was polished to gleaming perfection.

The house, the large garage, the potting shed, and the spring house sat on the northeastern edge of twenty-eight acres and had been in the Wayland family for more years than anyone could remember and before the turn of the century it was used only as a summer residence so the family could escape the heat of New York City where they lived in a splendid Gramercy Park townhouse. In 1901 they started to spend their summers in fashionable Bridgehampton on Long Island—all of the best families were vacationing in the Hamptons—and almost abandoned the house in Millersburg. Not that the house ever fell into disrepair: the family was too conscious of reputation to let that happen; they merely stopped going there. That was all back when there was Wayland money, most of which disappeared with the crash of '29. My grandfather, Byard Wayland, also disappeared with the crash and it was several years before his skeleton was discovered in the Jersey Pines with a bullet hole in the skull. The coroner's office finally decided it was self-inflicted because there was no evidence of foul play and there was a rusty revolver in his bony hand. He was identified by dental records. Mamu refused to discuss the discovery of the body and merely said that it came as no surprise. She was relieved that his remains were found because she wanted to put the legend of Byard Wayland to rest, who, since his disappearance, had been rumored to have done everything from running off with an heiress to the South China Sea to climbing Mount Everest. She never publicly mourned. For that matter, as far as we knew, she never privately mourned. In fact, she refused to have anything to do with his funeral, leaving my scattered, nervous, and chronically apologetic mother the unpleasant task of making all the arrangements to bury her father's skeleton. Under the circumstances, and with the help of my sister and me, she did very well, and the turnout at the cemetery was quite impressive, my grandfather having been well liked by everyone with the exception, it seemed, of my grandmother. Also, the suicide, the shattered skull, and all the other ghastly details, true or manufactured, spread through town like a field fire out of control and packed the church and graveyard to overflowing. Nothing drew so big a crowd in Millersburg as a good funeral. Especially if it was a funeral for someone who died of anything but natural causes and funerals for suicides were few and far between and, therefore, very well attended. Mother wore her favorite black dress, a single string of faux pearls, and an enormous picture hat which set off her fading tawny beauty and made her look like a cameo and because Mamu wasn't there to steal her thunder, for a change, she got all the attention from the assembled mourners, which clearly delighted her. No one has ever smiled so readily and ingratiatingly throughout a funeral. Because grandfather was a veteran of the Spanish-American War, having served with Dewey in the Philippines when the Spanish fleet was defeated, he was considered a hero and was buried accordingly. There was an honor guard and the ceremonial folding of the flag which was presented to my mother, who asked the sergeant at arms to give it to her a second time while she directed me to take another photo. Mother, no matter what the occasion was, took pictures of everything. There was a six-gun salute, which started every dog in town howling, and a painfully thin and sweaty soldier played a shaky and almost unrecognizable taps. There was hardly a dry eye at the gravesite. Except, of course, for mother, who tittered occasionally. Estella and I both thought Mamu should have been there, no matter how she felt about grandfather, because she was very partial to funerals and dearly loved spending time reading obituaries and occasionally visiting the cemetery. Since it was less than a mile from the house and within easy walking distance, when we were growing up Mamu dressed us in our best and sent us to many a funeral as entertainment, which Estella and I looked forward to as most children do going to a playground. We almost always brought a bouquet of carnations home for Mamu and mother, sometimes tied with a purple ribbon that had a brief but touching farewell message for the dearly departed. And we had two of our very rare family picnics amid the tombstones chronicling the comings and goings of the late Millersburg citizenry.

The largest monument, a triumphant archangel Gabriel, holding a lily in one hand, a trumpet in the other, wearing a flowing gown with long tresses and pursed lips that made him look as though he was about to whistle a tune or throw a kiss, marked the final resting place of Otto August Müller, a German immigrant after whom the town was named. It was originally Müllersburg but since he built the mill on Settlers Creek, the primary reason the town grew in the first place, and served as the only miller in the area for many years, Müller became Miller and the town became Millersburg. As long as he lived (he was 104 when he died) he was a member of a small and extremely unpopular German religious sect, the Josefites, which demanded absolute celibacy, and therefore he left no heirs to protest the name change. A basic tenet of the Josefites taught that when Christ came back he would be born to a celibate father as he had been the first time. Therefore, every male member of the sect was a possible foster father of the Son of God whenever the Second Coming happened. Oddly, there was never any talk about the women having a virgin birth. Everyone in Millersburg knew about the Josefites because their compound, consisting of several eerily empty red brick buildings; the women's dormitory and the men's dormitory on either side of the main hall, which served as a church and dining room, was one of the only two points of interest in the area and the very large and beautiful lake being the other. There was always talk of turning the stark, undefiled buildings into a resort hotel, even though it was about a mile from the lakeshore, but eventually it was placed on the historical registry and preserved as a landmark. The Josefites were also famous for making an elixir, Josef's Vasser, which was eighty proof alcohol and reputed to cure everything from hangnails to St. Vitus Dance. "Vasser" was misspelled, but I think the Josefites wanted it pronounced correctly. Nearly every home in New Jersey had a bottle of Josef's Vasser for medicinal purposes. Especially, said Mamu, the Methodists who preached that drinking alcohol was sinful. She had no time for the Methodists or any other religion for that matter. As a church, Josefism had a very short life. Less than a hundred years. But in that relatively short time they made a small fortune selling Josef's Vasser. No one ever knew what they did with the money and when the last Josefite was on his deathbed he kept mum and it was never found. The sect also preached frugality and simplicity and Mamu insisted that Herr Müller was spinning in his grave because of the outlandish and pretentious monument the town had lovingly and respectfully erected to his memory with money collected from people who couldn't even afford to put shoes on their children's feet.

It was supposed by most of the people attending grandfather's farewell service that Mamu was immobilized by grief and couldn't possibly get there when, in fact, she was at home canning dill pickles which she later said was unquestionably more important than the ridiculous show at the cemetery. Whenever my sister and I asked why she didn't like grandfather she said it was because he always cheated when they played chess and that if he wasn't winning, he quit. In all the years we lived with Mamu we never saw her play chess. There wasn't even a chess set in the house. It was a long time before we realized that playing chess was another of her metaphors. For living.

There were three other people who were part of the daily life in the big white house on Broadway. My uncle Joshua Pritchard, Mamu's much younger, by thirty-some years, half-brother, lived alone in a shack on Settlers Creek, which was the southwestern property line of our land. He was an educated man, a graduate of Princeton University, soft-spoken and almost courtly in manner, and who had no discernible ambitions. Uncle Josh spent all of his spare time reading so if anyone ever asked what he did for a living we simply said, "he reads." He did fish, maneuvering his rowboat, the Santa Maria, up and down Settlers Creek and out into Miller Lake with the ease and grace of a water spider, and during the winter he and I trapped muskrat and hunted. We also conspired against the McElway brothers, who had had the creek to themselves before we started trapping and, in retaliation, stole our traps even though we set them on our own land. The McElways were big and dumb and vicious, a result of inbreeding, according to Uncle Josh. It was a war that was constantly being waged against a silent, unseen, but ever-present enemy. We always referred to them as the rotten McElways or the Missing Links.

Uncle Josh helped with whatever chores Mamu assigned and when he focused his energies he was remarkably good at anything he tried but, whenever he could, he read. Fiction was his preference. He wasn't interested in history for history's sake but only as a background for a personal story in which characters prospered and lived or floundered and died. Economics, politics, religion, and philosophy merely provided the stages on which these comedies or dramas were performed.

And he wondered. He always wondered. "I wonder how many galaxies there are," or "I wonder if in some far-off place, the African bush, perhaps, where there are no musical instruments but rudimentary drums, if a child with the musical capabilities of a Mozart has been born only to wither and die unfulfilled, leaving no indication of his genius." Or "I wonder why birds don't fall off their perches when they fall asleep," and "I wonder if sex is anything more than friction and fantasy. That's not as simple as it sounds and doesn't preclude love. No, love is the essential ingredient. But the act of lovemaking is little more than friction and fantasy. The physical and the metaphysical. Certainly fantasy can be metaphysical, abstruse, and transcendent, especially where love is concerned. Friction and fantasy. I wonder." I don't know about Estella, but his wondering was contagious. And not only concerning sex and love. Because of him I fell asleep most nights wondering and I do to this day. And the older I get the more I realize there's never an end to the wondering.

Uncle Josh made magic for Estella and me. He opened doors to worlds we never would have known existed. His shack was one tidy room with no running water or electricity and no indoor plumbing, but the magic was on the walls. They were papered with overlapping maps with pins stuck in certain landmarks or cities and circles drawn around others. Every shade of pink and green and blue and yellow and orange brightened the room. I remember the Soviet Union was a harsh and unexpected vibrant red, making it difficult to read the names of the cities and villages. Maps of the world, maps of New Jersey, maps of Europe, Asia, Africa, Australia, maps of islands, maps of oceans, and maps of the heavens, all tantalizing in a collage that was meant to seduce the dreamer. Uncle Josh was one and so was Estella. I, on the other hand, although I certainly was capable of flights of fancy, was basically practical. Perhaps realistic is a better word. Maybe that was because I didn't want to get my hopes up. Realism seemed so much more palatable than disappointment. But Estella and Uncle Josh were willing to take their chances.

"Some day I'm going to go to Algeria to the Tassili Mountains," he'd say, obviously savoring the word "Tassili" and pointing to a cir-cled spot in the middle of the Sahara desert. "There are wall paintings there that are three . . . maybe four thousand years old. I want to see them. I want to stand in the middle of that bleak and beautiful mountain range and look at paintings that someone was compelled to create two thousand years before Christ was born." He was enrap-tured. "And someday I'm going to ride the Trans-Siberian Railroad. It starts in Chelyabinsk and ends in Vladivostok. What wonderful names for cities that I'm sure are full of wonder." He could hardly contain himself once he started. "You see that?" He indicated a tiny dot with two pins sticking in it. "That's Persepolis. The ruins of the palace of Darius the Great are there. And this, this was one of the most important Ionian cities in the ancient world. Ephesus. I'm going there some day. Maybe to live. It was the leading seaport in the region. Sophisticated and wealthy beyond imagining. I can close my eyes and picture what it was like. I want to walk the streets of Ephesus some day." Uncle Josh's life was full of "somedays."

I suppose it was difficult enough for him to live in a shack with an outhouse for a toilet and pretend it was a palace, which he often did, so he had nothing to lose and, therefore, realism had no place in his life. He washed in the creek in the summer when he and Estella and I, without Mamu and Eulalie knowing, went skinny-dipping when our work was finished for the day. It was as idyllic and innocent as Eden before the fall, the three of us naked as eggs, splashing in the cool brackish water, but Mamu would have made something nasty of it and forbidden us to go to Uncle Josh's shack and that was as important to the survival of our souls as food is to the body. If we managed to get to the creek early enough, especially in midsummer when the light lasted the longest, after we had renewed and exhausted ourselves swimming, we stretched out on the little boat dock, like turtles basking on a log, and dried in the warm air as we listened to records on his wind-up Victrola. "Mozart is the icing on the cake," he'd say. "There never was and there never will be another like little Wolfgang Amadeus. But then, of course, there's Liszt. Franz was no slouch. The Second Hungarian Rhapsody. Oh, my! All that passion and sensuality and humor in one magnificent composition. And what about Schumann and his Clara?" Schumann and his wife Clara were almost one word. Schumannandhisclara. "And poor, unhappy Tchaikovsky and crazy old Beethoven? Luckily, we don't really have to choose, do we?" Or if we were in the mood we'd listen to Louis Armstrong and His Hot Five playing "Heeby Jeebies" or "Don't Forget To Mess Around." Sometimes, he read to us. He was a wonderful reader, energetic and colorful, bringing all the characters so clearly to life I could almost see them standing in the deep shadow of the trees along the banks, like actors waiting in the wings to go on stage.

In the winter, when the water in the creek was too cold and often frozen, he had his bath on Saturday night up at the house. He had dinner with us every evening and, when Mamu was disposed to listen, told us fascinating, truncated versions of some of the world's great literature and so we shared the table with the likes of Tolstoy and Irving, Twain and Dostoevski, the Brontës and Dickens. Unlike Mamu, who was short and solid with cold green eyes and frizzy, reddish hair like her mother's family, Uncle Josh was tall and lean with olive skin, dark, graying hair, and clear, inquisitive blue eyes. He resembled the tintype I had seen of my great-grandfather. And he had the same coloring as Estella and me. She was two years older, but we looked enough alike to be twins and when strangers saw us with Uncle Josh they assumed he was our father. Mamu said our darkness came from a mysterious female ancestor on her grandfather's side named Immaculata DeLago who was swept under the rug with several other of her forebearers. They weren't the kind of people one discussed in polite society. Or, at least, they weren't the kind of people anyone in her family discussed because she really knew very little about Immaculata except that her genes imprinted dramatically on the family. Her theory was that "the DeLago woman" was anything but immaculate and was unquestionably a prostitute. This delighted Estella and me.

The details of how Uncle Josh came to actually live in Millersburg with my grandparents were sketchy. Originally, he must have stayed in the house—there were six bedrooms—but how and when he moved to the shack on the creek we never knew. He was the only child of my great-grandfather's second marriage to a woman younger than Mamu, who died suddenly from influenza when Uncle Josh was a baby. He and my mother were almost the same age. When he was a boy it was discovered that he suffered from tuberculosis and he was sent to a sanitarium in Arizona for several years and was completely cut off from the family. We always thought his love of books, his astonishing ability to lose himself in the worlds between the covers, was a result of his isolation. He regained his health, but because of the illness wasn't able to serve in the army during the First World War. His father, my great-grandfather, died when Uncle Josh was thirteen, but left a small trust that saw him through his years at Princeton. After college, his apparent lack of direction and his dismal financial state must have triggered some familial responsibility in Mamu and she took him in. Apparently, grandfather didn't object. Certainly, it was meant to be a temporary arrangement. I don't think Mamu's charity was motivated by any degree of sisterly love because there were times when she seemed to barely tolerate him and treated him as a servant. His obvious lack of ambition and his eagerness to withdraw to the privacy of his shack on the creek annoyed Mamu and she often let him know it. If he minded, he never said anything. We all complained about Mamu, in one way or another, but he said little or nothing by way of actual criticism. I think he was grateful to have someplace to live and a place where, for the most part, he was left to his own devices: his music and his books and maps. And the water. He loved being on the water and knew the creek and lake as intimately as I knew the house. On summer nights when we would glide silently along the shore gigging frogs (Mamu was particularly fond of frog's legs), we hardly needed a lantern.

Although Uncle Josh was a spellbinder, who could paint wonderful pictures with words and captivate Estella and me with his incredible stories, he was also a very private man who, like the rest of the household, said nothing about what he was really feeling. Feelings were superfluous in the world created by Mamu and that was the world in which we all resided, somewhat obsequiously. Mamu saw to that. No tyrant ever ruled with a firmer and more merciless hand than she did. Feelings were off-limits. Living was about responsibility and responsibility was clear-cut and obvious and if we couldn't quite delineate what our responsibilities were Mamu was there to do it for us. And so, our feelings were our private property to be dealt with alone in the emptiness of our rooms and the dark corners of our minds as best we could. Consequently, we lived in a house of shadowy secrets.

The other members of the household were Priddie and Osceola Flowers. Priddie was the daughter of young slaves freed at the end of the Civil War and Osceola was the son of a slave who had been freed even before the war started by his abolitionist owner. Priddie was born in Louisiana and Osceola was from Georgia. His mother was a Seminole woman who named her only son after the revered and legendary Jim Osceola, the great Seminole resistance leader who was captured only because he trusted the word of the white government and attended a truce meeting where he was taken prisoner. One of the most heinous acts of cowardice and deception in recorded time, according to Osceola Flowers, and the reason the Seminole nation never signed a peace treaty with the United States. He was clearly a black man, sturdy and well proportioned, but his hair was straight and thick, and his nose and cheekbones all attested to his Indian heritage. Priddie adored him, but said she only married him so that she could go through life as Priddie Flowers. She was very dark, graceful and seemingly fragile, but was as strong as any ten men. Her hair was gray and thinning and her great amber eyes, sad even when she laughed, seemed too big for her elegant face. Mamu said she was the only real lady she had ever met. There was always the faint and sweetish aroma of herbs about her like one of her just brewed special teas. Priddie had had five pregnancies, four of which ended in miscarriage. She finally gave birth to a daughter, Camille, but according to Priddie, "she wasn't right." On occasion, Camille would come to the house with her parents, especially to help with canning, but she usually stayed in the kitchen and said little or nothing. She was a nondescript girl: not tall or short, dark or light, fat or thin, lovely or plain. She was just there. Estella and I would try to lure her outside but she wouldn't budge, silent and secure with her mother nearby. The Flowers had a small house on the other side of Millersburg in what we called Brick Town, or "the colored section," the center of which was the First Baptist Church of the Nazarene. If anyone in our family was sick or needed Priddie or Osceola to stay over for any reason, one or the other would sleep on the divan in Mamu's sewing room. Never in one of the bedrooms. I didn't know if that was Mamu's rule or the Flowers' preference. But, at night, one of them always had to be at home with the peculiar and almost invisible Camille. There was a mystery woman we knew very little about who looked after Camille during the day. Estella and I saw her several times at the house but we never spoke to her. Priddie said she didn't feel right leaving Camille alone and alluded to her being less than capable of looking after herself, but didn't go into detail no matter how much Estella and I tried to get her to discuss it.

"I just wish she could find a man," she'd say. "She wants a baby. She wants a baby real bad. But it ain't lookin' too good for that. Her bein' as strange as she is."

Mamu told us to mind our own business and leave Priddie to her work.

We never thought of Priddie and Osceola as servants. The truth was, many a year went by without their receiving a penny in wages. There just wasn't any money until Mamu and Osceola started a business together. In the beginning there was the pittance my mother brought in from her secretarial job which, against all odds, she managed to hold onto at Schiller's lumberyard, in Laurelwood, eighteen miles from Millersburg. Eulalie took the bus every morning at 6:30 and if she worked late didn't get home until 11:00 at night. In the cold weather, if there was a heavy snow, she'd either stay over at the hotel in Laurelwood or phone and Osceola would pick her up at the bus stop in town in his old Model T truck. The only freedom she had was being away from home and Estella and I were certain she worked as late as she could on purpose.

Eventually, the Flowers were given a percentage of the money that came in. That was before Mamu made Osceola a partner in the business. I don't think she did it because it was the honorable thing to do. She did it because she couldn't abide being beholden to anyone. Financially or emotionally. And also because she respected them. The circumstances of the Depression necessitated her dependence on Priddie and Osceola and Mamu knew that if it wasn't for them they never would have started their own business and we never would have survived those impossibly hard years. It was the combination of their know-how and determination, Osceola and Mamu's, sometimes at the expense of everyone in the family, that saved us.

There was one other presence in the house. Not in body but in spirit. My father. There were no pictures of him and his name was never mentioned when Mamu was present, but he was always there and one way or another we were constantly reminded of him even if it was only in what we saw in mother's eyes. Like a martyr to a cause, he was a much more imposing figure in his absence than he ever could have been had he lived with us. Devlin Whyte was the great love of my mother's life and Mamu had driven him away. She didn't want mother to marry him in the first place and did everything she could to stop the wedding, agreeing only when she discovered my mother was pregnant with Estella. It was a quiet little service with only family members in attendance. Mother's premature pregnancy was another dark secret in the family, the source of rage and embarrassment for Mamu, and it fueled the hatred she already felt for my father. I remembered him vaguely, as a tall ghostly presence that smelled of pipe tobacco and bay rum, because I was only three when he left. But Estella was almost five and her memory of him was startlingly clear, if wildly diverse, depending on the day or mood she was in. Sometimes he was tall and dark as Uncle Josh with mysterious eyes "that could burn a hole in a person." Or he might be pale and golden as a summer day, flawless and warm and available. But dark or fair, he was always astonishingly handsome. There were times when she talked about his glorious singing voice and his remarkable grace on the dance floor. He was also a crack shot with a rifle, an indefatigable swimmer, a formidable tennis player, an expert on a polo pony, an accomplished pianist, a fine painter, and he could run as fast as the wind. His hair was thick and glossy, his nose was regally straight and well proportioned, and his teeth were perfectly even, white as bleached bone.

He was always appropriately and exceptionally well dressed no matter what the occasion was. When I allowed myself the freedom of fancy I believed everything she said. I certainly wanted to because I needed to put a face on him. She remembered him holding our mother in his arms and kissing her, gently at first but, invariably, the kisses became passionate embraces, which always led to their going upstairs and closing their bedroom door. One of those encounters, she reminded me, resulted in my conception, but she wasn't quite sure she remembered which one. After all, she was only two at the time. The stories were almost as good as the stories Uncle Josh told and didn't lose interest for me because I was always curious as to which incarnation Estella would have our father appear in. Alone, I spent many an hour speculating on his whereabouts or whether or not he was even alive. When I was away from Estella my mind was clear and all the things she said about him faded away. He was still just the ghostly recollection that smelled of pipe tobacco and bay rum. But I felt that if I didn't really know him I didn't know myself and so, I thought, I was destined to be a stranger in my own skin and it was frightening. This caused me to have recurring nightmares in which I was in the circus, faceless, my body nothing more than wisps of some kind of nameless vapor walking a tight rope, trying to define myself, attempting to put edges on the gossamer me. But no matter how hard I tried I was indefinable, elusive, and unreachable.

I was my father's namesake, but I never remember being called Devlin. Someone, I later discovered it was Mamu, decided I'd be Ben and Ben I've always been. For years I wondered who I was named after but, for whatever reason, I never asked. When, finally, I did, Mamu said that when my father left she had been reading a tattered old copy of *Ben Hur* and she never wanted to hear the name Devlin again so I became Ben. It was that simple. That simple and that ridiculous. Had she been reading the *Odyssey*, I might possibly have gone through life being called Odysseus or Telemachus.

I did have the comfort of knowing my father was a good man. At least that was what Osceola and Priddie told me. They were forbidden to talk about him and whenever the subject came up, when Mamu wasn't around, they would dismiss it but always made a point of saying, "he is a good man." Any mention of him, however, seemed to make them uncomfortable. Uncle Josh said, "He's a man with big dreams who just keeps stubbing his toe on them." Then he'd smile and say, "Some of us have a hard time finding ourselves." The fact that Uncle Josh likened himself to my father helped to define him slightly in my mind and I was certain that he was "a good man."

Chapter II

"You don't have to go back to school this fall," said Mamu as she was sorting the eggs into baskets for large, medium, and small. We were in the little room off the hen house where we did the candling. The chickens had been let out for the morning and were scratching and squabbling as they went after bugs. Even that early in the morning it was already too warm and sultry to breathe. Mamu mopped her brow with her apron.

"But I want to finish high school. Estella finished high school. I want to go to college someday."

"And do what? What do you want to go to college for?" She had no respect for education. I always thought it was because she could have gone on to college after high school, but chose to stay home with her mother who was ill by that time. It was a sacrifice she didn't have to make. There was plenty of money for nurses, but she used the illness as an excuse not to continue her education and had contempt for people who did. "You don't need college to run this place. I'll be dead before summer ends. . . ." I started to protest but she shut me up. "I will and that's all there is to it. I'm getting off the carousel and it's about time. I'm almost seventy years old. That's an old woman. I don't want to get sick and feeble so I've decided to go."

"Mamu, you can't just decide to die. . . ."

"Piffle! I can. And I will. Don't tell me what I can or cannot do!" She took a deep breath and brushed away a moth that had been pestering her. "You'll have to take care of everything after I'm gone. Who do you think I built this business for? Your mother? Your mother is useless and you know it. And sooner or later Estella will run off and get married. If Adam Stoner has anything to say about it it will be sooner than later."

Adam was in love with Estella and used any excuse he could to come to the house just to get a look at her. Mamu usually made it perfectly clear that he wasn't welcome. He was a sheriff's deputy, tall, slim, fair and very impressive in his uniform. He was almost five years older than Estella, and as long as I could remember he had been coming around on the flimsiest excuses, usually weather related. Although Estella didn't admit it she was thrilled to see his car coming down Broadway. And so was I. "A bad storm's coming. I thought you people ought to know." He usually stayed in the car for the first moment or two, waiting to see if Mamu would come charging out of the house, as unpleasant as her bad manners dictated. Then he'd open the door, unfold his long legs, and stretch as though he had been driving for hours. If I was there he always shook hands with me first, saving Estella, the good part of the visit, for last. "Looks like we're going to have a drought." He never seemed to sweat. At most, his face might glisten from the heat. "Snow's supposed to be about two feet deep. I'll drop by to see if you need help clearing your road, OK?" No matter what he said everyone knew, especially Estella, that he was only there to see her. She obviously enjoyed the attention, but if I asked how she felt about him she told me to "mind my own bee's wax."

"Girls do that. They run off and get married." Mamu wiped the beads of perspiration off her upper lip. "Even to a man like Adam Stoner. What future has he, I ask you? A sheriff's deputy! And his nose is too big. Young girls can be so stupid. They think that's the answer to everything. A man! So foolish. Especially girls like Estella."

I didn't like Estella being lumped with other girls in one of Mamu's contemptuous generalizations. She wasn't foolish and she certainly wasn't stupid. I assumed she meant because Estella was so pretty. Pretty girls like her run off and get married. But there were no girls like her. There was only one Estella.

"And you'll have to look after your Uncle Josh. He's not good for much. I think he's as crazy as a loon."

"He's not crazy. Why do you always. . . ."

"All right, he's not crazy. You don't have to get into a huff every time his name is mentioned. But whatever's wrong with him he probably gets from that Spanish woman. She was bad blood." She shook her head in annoyance. "You'll have Priddie and Osceola to help . . . they're getting old but they're strong. They'll be around for a few more years. The colored seem to last longer than us. I don't know why that is. No matter, you'll have to run things."

"But I want to finish school and go to college," I repeated.

"A lot of good college did your Uncle Josh. He knew how to read before he got there and that's all that interests him. A liberal arts education. How ridiculous!" She said it as though she was talking about a contagious disease.

"But. . . ."

"What do you want to do that you have to go to college? Tell me. Can you tell me that? I'd like to know."

I didn't know what I wanted to do. All I knew was that I wanted to go someplace else. I was born in that house and I never spent one single night away from it. Not one night. There was a whole world beyond Millersburg, a world that in my mind was blue and pink and orange and had pins stuck in it. I wanted to go to every place Uncle Josh had circled on his maps. To Ephesus. To the Tassili Mountains in the middle of the Sahara. To places where I could meet strangers who might become my friends. Where I could get to know people. People who weren't family. There were limitless possibilities. I wanted to get away from working until I was ready to drop, from Mamu's rules, from Mamu's demands, from Mamu herself.

"You think college is a ticket to an easy life? Well, let me tell you it isn't."

"No. I didn't say that. Did I say I wanted an easy life?"

"Don't get smart with me," she scolded.

"But there are some things I'd like to do."

"Well, tell me."

"I'm not exactly sure."

"When you are sure, we'll discuss your going to college. Right now, take the eggs down to the stand. Osceola's waiting for you. He's got better things to do than sit there all morning. He's got deliveries to make. Estella will relieve you at lunch time."

"I really want to finish school, Mamu. . . ."

"Fine. You go to college and I'll give the business to Osceola and Priddie."

"I didn't say I didn't want the business." But I didn't.

"Then we'll talk about it later." The conversation concerning school was over. "What kind of cake do you want for your birthday?"

It was typical of Mamu to change the topic of conversation to something that she thought would make her look like a reasonable and caring person. Suddenly she was showing concern. It was as close as she could get to any kind of warmth and even that was a ploy. No one ever believed her for a single moment.

"I don't care."

"Don't pout, Ben. You know how unattractive pouting is? And stand up straight. A man is judged on how straight he stands. Now, what kind of cake do you want? I have to tell Priddie."

"Chocolate," I said, not caring if I even had a cake, let alone what kind it was.

"Fine. Chocolate." She sighed, obviously annoyed.

"What about the World's Fair?" My birthday present that year was to have been a trip to the World's Fair. It was mentioned once, at Christmas time when Mamu had a glass of sherry.

"What about it?"

"You said we were going. For my birthday."

"It's ridiculous. The world is on the brink of disaster and they're having a fair."

"Maybe it will bring people together. That's what it's meant to do, isn't it?"

"What it's meant to do and what it will do are two different things. What do you know? You're so naïve."

I hated being dismissed by, "What do you know?"

"I'd still like to go."

"Who wants to go to New York in this heat? Do you know how far Flushing Meadows is?

"So, we're not going. . . ?"

"I didn't say that. Don't go putting words in my mouth. Maybe in the fall when it cools down. How long is it on?"

"Until the end of October."

"And it'll be next summer, right?"

"Yes."

"Then what's the rush? We'll talk about it later. Now get moving with these eggs before they hard-boil in this heat."

I picked up the baskets and left the hen house and I could hear her clucking to herself as loudly as the chickens. I started down Broadway toward the stand and two mourning doves, picking in the dirt, shot into the sky, their wings whistling as they disappeared over a maple tree. How easy, I thought, it was for them to simply fly away. I felt like a prisoner who had just been condemned to life. Mamu had made up her mind that I was finished with my schooling and that I'd take care of the place until the end of my days and that was that. There would be no discussion later.

"We're out of pennies," said Osceola as I arrived at the stand. "I'll ask your grandmother for some and bring 'em down to you later. You're goin' to need 'em." It was Saturday and the weekends were our busiest times because we were on a direct route to the ocean and we had a lot of people going and coming from the summer resorts at the shore. He took one of the baskets of eggs from me. "What's wrong with them hens? Must be too hot for them to lay. Keep them in the shade so they stay fresher." He had everything displayed perfectly, as always. He had been there since six in the morning just in case there was an early customer. The first corn of the season was stacked neatly next to the squash and cantaloupes and tomatoes and cucumbers and there was a basket of green beans filled to overflowing. Even though it was mid-summer, because of Osceola's staggered planting, there were still spring onions and radishes. The jams, preserves, pickles, relishes, and jars of honey were arranged perfectly on the shelves along with the little packets of dried herbs and there were buckets of water stuffed with cock's comb, gladioli, daisies, and black-eyed Susans. Priddie had picked them just after sunup that morning.

"People might be hard up for cash, but they always find a little to buy flowers," she'd say. "It makes bad times a little easier, I reckon."

She had also potted some herb seedlings in old tin cans and they were arranged as neatly as plants in a flower shop.

"What's wrong with you, boy? You look like the dog died or somethin'." Osceola put a cloth over the eggs to shade them.

"We don't have a dog."

"I know we ain't got a dog. I'm just sayin' that's what you look like. What's wrong with you?"

"Nothing." I didn't feel like talking about it.

"Miz Adela getting you down? Hell, you should a got used to that by now. Just don't pay no mind to her when she gets mean. How many times I have to say that? I been telling Priddie that for years. Just don't pay no mind to her when she gets mean." Osceola repeated things when he wanted to emphasize. "But you know Priddie. Sometimes she's like granite and other times she's as fragile as a hummingbird's egg, gettin' all hurt and all. Miz Adela can be the meanest white woman in the state of New Jersey, but just don't pay her no mind."

"I don't want to talk about it."

"Do you good to talk about it, boy. I think it would. You know I'm a good listener. I been listenin' to you jammerin' on since you was born. Since you first saw the light of day."

"All the talking in the world isn't going to do me any good." I looked up and down the highway, but there wasn't a car in sight. "Anybody been by?"

"Yeah. I sold a dozen ears of corn to one man. Never seen him before. Didn't recognize the car, neither. Had a bunch of kids in it. On their way to the shore I guess. Never seen him before in my life." He was in love with all things automotive and knew every car and every owner in Millersburg.

"You go on and do whatever you have to do and I'll be OK here." I ducked under the counter.

"It's goin' to be a hot one. Even the flies is takin' it easy. You stay in the shade, you hear me, boy?"

"I'll be fine."

"I'll bring the pennies down later." He started up Broadway. "I got a busy day ahead of me. I got the deliveries to make and I got to take Masha to be freshened. She come into season early. And you know how particular Miz Adela is about them ladies. She kill me if I don't do for 'em exactly the way she wants." Masha was one of our three goats that was in heat and ready to be taken to the only Saanan buck in the area, belonging to a farmer on the road to Laurelwood. Our other two goats were Irina and Olga, Uncle Josh was reading Chekhov when we got them. Osceola wasn't very happy with the highfalutin names because he was thinking along the lines of Daisy and Buttercup, but Uncle Josh won and in no time at all we took our goats with the Russian names for granted and in the ensuing years all of our nanny goats were named either Masha, Irina, or Olga.

"I hate bein' away for the day. Them two boys workin' the fields ain't worth spit. I can't understand a word they sayin'. Talking that Hungarian or Polish or what ever the hell it is."

"Hungarian. And they have names. Stash and Janos."

"Seems the only English they know is the 'F' word."

"Fuck!" It was the first time I ever said the word aloud and it was surprisingly rich and explosive and satisfying.

"Whoa. . . ." Osceola was wide-eyed. "You don't go sayin' that word around the ladies, you hear? That's a man's word. Sometimes there ain't no other word to take its place. But if Priddie hears you say it she's goin' to blame me and I don't want to think what Miz Adela would do. Makes my blood run cold."

"Fuck Mamu!" I said it and I suddenly got a queasiness in my stomach. I felt like I had done something I would have to pay for as long as I lived. Something dreadful and irreversible like shooting her right in the heart.

"You jumpin' in all at once, ain't you boy? Fuck Miz Adela. I thought about sayin' it myself many times, that's the truth. I guess I just ain't the man you are." He smiled broadly. "I would like to know what the hell is possessin' you this mornin'."

"Never mind."

"You in a bad way, I know that much."

"Go do what you have to do."

"I'll check up on the foreigners. Maybe it's goin' to take time for 'em to catch on. The big one ain't so bad. I can't say nothin' to Miz Adela or she march right out in the field and fire their useless asses on the spot. And I got to find some time for my truck today, too. It stops runnin', we're out of luck." He turned to me. "Why won't Miz Adela let me get that old car in the barn runnin'? Somebody has got to get it into her thick head that we need that car. It don't make a bit a sense to me."

It was the same question we had all been asking for almost ten years. Grandfather's Cadillac Phaeton was up on blocks in the barn, a perfectly good car as far as we knew, and Mamu wouldn't let anyone near it. It just sat there collecting dust. No one had driven it since grandfather disappeared. Whenever we asked her about it she walked away, refusing to discuss it, or she told us it was none of our concern. I had been driving on country roads, thanks to Osceola, since I was eleven and into town on errands by myself since I was fifteen. But, when I turned seventeen I would get my official license and I wanted the car more than anyone.

"Forget it," I said. "You know better than to even think about it."

"It don't make no sense at all. Or why don't we buy a new truck. A new truck with *Broadway Acres, The Best Tomatoes in New Jersey* printed on the side. We got the money. Shit, we got more than enough money. And it pays to advertise. Everybody knows that. It pays to advertise. *The Best Tomatoes in New Jersey.* Then maybe we have a silhouette of a chorus girl, big titties and nice long legs and a big behind. You get it? The best tomatoes?"

"Yes, I get it. Tomatoes . . . girls . . . I get it. OK? You think I'm stupid?"

"No, I don't think you're stupid, but you sure are one mean little son-of-a-bitch. You just watch your mouth when you talkin' to me. I been wastin' my time tryin' to make a man of you, I can see that. You just want to stay a whiny little white boy, that's fine with me."

"Mamu wants me to quit school." Osceola always knew how to wear me down.

"Is that what all this fuss is about? Hell, I thought it was somethin' important. She got a feather up her ass is all. Don't you worry about her. You ain't quittin' school and that's all there is to it. I'll see to that. No sir, you ain't quittin' school."

It was reassuring having Osceola on my side, but Mamu was a force to be reckoned with.

"What was we talking about. . . . Oh, yeah, gettin' a new truck. Hell, we could afford two new trucks. But Miz Adela is tighter than a size nine shoe on a size twelve foot." Osceola started up the road again. "Roll down that canopy, boy," he yelled over his shoulder. "You don't need the sunstroke, you know. It's goin' to be hotter than a skunk's nest today. Hotter than a damn skunk's nest." He stopped and turned. "Don't you think no more about that school business. I take care of that. You hear? And one more thing. You watch your language. You slip and say the 'F' word in front of the wrong person and it's goin' to be my black ass that gets fried. No wonder you said fuck Miz Adela. Lord amighty." He shook his head, started to chuckle, and went on his way, leaving me in my misery.

Chapter III

We heard about the murders on the radio the morning of August 30th, the day before my birthday, when we were having breakfast. It was humid and enervating, so oppressive that everyone was slightly edgy. We were listening to *Rambling with Gambling* as we did every weekday morning. It was Mamu's favorite program and so, of course, that's what we listened to even though we paid little or no attention to Mr. Gambling. Half the time Mamu didn't pay any attention, either, as she read the morning paper, checking the obituaries. There was a news bulletin and all the announcer said was that a spokesman for the Millersburg, New Jersey police had reported two bodies discovered in a cottage on Miller Lake and that it was apparently a double murder. The names were being withheld until notification of family.

"Millersburg! Did you hear that? My God, a murder in Millers–burg." I couldn't believe it.

"Two murders," said Estella.

"Oh, my Lord!" Priddie was aghast.

"Well, it doesn't surprise me," said Mamu, folding the paper and pouring herself a second cup of coffee. The milking was done and she could relax for a few minutes. "Those summer people . . . well, it just doesn't surprise me, that's all."

"You don't even know any of the summer people." Estella was helping Priddie with the dishes. "Why would you say a thing like that?"

"No matter who got killed," said Priddie, "it's a terrible thing. Lord have mercy."

"All I'm saying is, it doesn't surprise me."

This was the most conversation we had had at the breakfast table in years. Usually we were told what we had to do that day and then we sat in silence while we ate and listened to the radio. I didn't want the exchange to end. "Are they the first murders in town?"

"Of course not." She poured some cream in her cup. "We've had several murders in Millersburg. A couple of good ones, too. Most of them when you two were just kids. There was a man who beat another man to death with a crowbar. The murdered man was a banker. And a Republican. Can't remember his name. But the murderer was Roger something. . . ."

"Rhodes," added Priddie. "Mr. Roger Rhodes."

"That's it. Roger Rhodes. The banker wouldn't give him a loan. I think that's what it was. It was just at the start of the Depression and the man, Mr. Rhodes, was going to lose his home. As it happened, it didn't matter because Mr. Roger Rhodes was electrocuted in Trenton. I never did think it was a capital crime to kill a Republican. And, Priddie, what was the name of that woman who blew her husband's head off?"

"You mean Miz Popovic?"

"Eloise Popovic's mother shot her father?" asked Estella.

"No, no. Eloise Popovic's grandmother shot her grandfather."

"I never heard that," said Estella. "Eloise never said anything."

"Well, it's not the kind of thing you brag to your friends about, is it?" For some odd reason Mamu laughed.

Priddie shook her head. "It was such a terrible thing. And him with one leg shorter than the other. Remember his short leg, Miz Adela? I heard he was on the *Titanic* and his leg got hurt when he jumped."

"Victor Popovic wasn't on the *Titanic*. Where on earth did you hear that?"

"I don't rightly remember." Priddie cocked her head as she usually did when she was trying to remember something.

"Piffle! Victor Popovic has never been out of Millersburg, for Lord's sake. On the *Titanic*! That's the most ridiculous thing I ever heard. You'd believe the moon was made of green cheese."

"Well, I didn't make it up."

"Honestly! How could you believe such a silly thing?"

"Why'd she shoot him?" I interjected, trying to get back to the point. I didn't give a damn about the *Titanic*.

Mamu wasn't going to let go of it. "Anyway, his short leg had nothing to do with her shooting his head off," she said. "Why'd you bring that short leg up? Who gives a fig about his short leg?"

"I'm not sayin' it did have anythin' to do with her shootin' his head off. I just remembered the man had one leg shorter than the other, that's all. Maybe he wasn't on the *Titanic*."

"He was bald, too. That didn't have anything to do with the murder, either."

"Well, excuse me for livin'. I just said the poor man had one leg shorter than the other." She turned to Estella and me. "His wife, Miz Popovic, was a very nice woman. Hard to believe she'd blow her husband's head off. Just no tellin' about people, is there?" Then, without looking at Mamu, "Am I allowed to say that?"

"Why?" I asked again, "I mean why'd she shoot him?"

"He had a lady friend." Mamu leaned in confidentially. "When a woman kills a man you can bet he's got a lady friend on the side. It happens all the time. Of course, most women are clever enough not to get caught. Rat poison or pushing him in front of a train or down a flight of stairs . . . things like that. Or making it look like a suicide." She smiled broadly. "I'll wager half the men who die of accidental deaths in this country are killed by their wives. I hear French women do it a lot more than we do. Of course, the French are more passionate about everything." Mamu was having a wonderful time.

"I think women are stronger than men, don't you, Priddie? Well, I know they are."

"Miz Adela, what is all this talk about killin'? Don't say things like that. Women folk killin' their husbands! What is wrong with you?"

"You ever wonder about your grandfather's death?" Mamu took a sip of her coffee while the question sank in.

Estella almost dropped the dish she was drying. "What?"

Priddie took a step toward Mamu. "Miz Adela, you stop this nonsense right now. You got the devil in you this mornin'!"

The murders had energized Mamu and she was almost glowing as she sat, grinning, having just implied that she shot her husband.

I couldn't believe it. "You shot grandfather?"

"The Lord will strike you dead if you say one more word of this foolishness." I had never seen Priddie stand up to Mamu like that. "What a terrible thing to go sayin' to the children. You shot Mr. Byard! What is wrong with you?"

"They're not children anymore. Ben is going to be seventeen and Estella's a woman." It wasn't unusual for Mamu to talk about us as though we weren't in the room, but it was unusual to talk about us as adults. Somehow it seemed to suggest that she was about to tell us something she had saved until we were grown up. The fact that she had murdered our grandfather.

"That ain't got nothin' to do with it. Whether they be grown up or not. You should be ashamed of yourself, Miz Adela." Priddie went back to the sink.

"Did you shoot Grandfather?" I asked again.

"What do you think?" There was a rare twinkle in her eye.

"Well . . . Mamu!" I didn't know what to think. "Why would you say that?"

"Ben, don't pay no mind to her." Priddie was getting more and more upset.

"Just having a little fun with you." Mamu left the table and went to the sink. "Don't get yourself all in a lather, Priddie."

"There ain't nothin' fun about talk like that. Nothin'. You been in the sherry, Miz Adela, or what? Awful early for that, ain't it? Sayin' stuff like that to the children. You know it just ain't the truth."

"I'm going out to the goats. Maybe they have a better sense of humor than you people." She poured herself a bit more coffee and without saying another word, left the kitchen. We were speechless.

"I don't understand that woman," said Priddie. "She ain't exactly famous for makin' fun, now, is she?"

"What was that about?" Estella flopped down in a chair across the table from me. "I've never seen her like that."

It had been a rare flash of a woman we didn't know, so peculiar to us that she could have come from another planet.

"I'm tellin' you right now, there ain't a word of truth in what your grandmother just said. Not a word. So, you just get it out of your minds. You hear me?"

But for the first time since I knew her I didn't quite believe Priddie. I had asked Mamu point blank if she had killed grandfather and she didn't say no. No matter what I did the rest of the day I couldn't get the idea of Mamu killing him out of my mind. Violent death, especially murder, was something that happened in the movies. Not that we ever saw very many because Mamu didn't approve. "It's a waste of time," she'd say whenever Estella and I wanted to go to the Rivoli in Laurelwood. "Why do you want to go to the moving pictures when you've got a perfectly good radio to listen to?"

Until the murders, death to me had simply been a kind of disappearance. Grandfather had disappeared and my father, whom I had come to believe was dead, had also disappeared. There was a boy in my freshman class, Thomas Wrennit, who was always sickly and died of polio, but even he disappeared. One day he was in school and then he was gone and we never saw him again. Or death was old people in town, people I really didn't know, people whose obituary Mamu read at the breakfast table. People whose funerals Estella and I attended when we were little. It was nature taking its course. But murder was something else. It was a death caused by a deliberate act. I couldn't get the horrifying idea of that out of my mind.

Estella and I wanted the details of the murders so she called the sheriff's office to talk to Adam, but the line was tied up and she didn't get through until almost five o'clock that evening, and when she did, Margaret Breedlove, who worked in the office, told her that Adam and the sheriff hadn't been in all day. They were at the scene of the crime. Estella and I had our heads together listening to whatever Margaret had to say. She usually provided more information to anyone who would listen to her than the *Millersburg Daily Reminder*. Working for the sheriff she was in a position to be, as she put it, "informed." Until the murders most of her information was about who spent the night in jail for drunkenness, who beat up his wife or who beat up her husband, and which kid got caught stealing penny candy from the Mercantile.

"The press is crawling all over Millersburg like flies on horse manure because the murder victims are rich and famous but," she suddenly got very professional, "I'm afraid I am not at liberty to divulge their names. Part of my job, don't you know. I never heard of either one of them so even if I spilled the beans you probably wouldn't know who they are. But, I don't listen to high-class music and the murdered man is a violinist or a flute player or maybe he plays the accordion . . . something like that. Very, very, very famous, though. And," she almost whispered, "the woman is not his wife. She's married to some rich man. Very rich man. Mrs. Richbitch. Well, you can expect anything from people with that kind of money. Not that I pass judgment on anybody. You know me better than that. You don't breathe a word of what I'm saying to anybody, you promise? About her not being his wife, I mean. I could lose my job. 'Course, I don't know how they'd get along around here without me. Word is, she was very beautiful and he was a Greek god. They're thinking hanky-panky between the two of them, but I'm not allowed to say anything. I'll only tell you this much. It was a bloodbath. Sheriff said he almost threw up. Well, I have to go," she said cheerily. "Members of the press just came in. I think they want to take my picture." She became very businesslike again. "You want me to have Adam call you?"

"Please," said Estella and hung up.

Adam didn't call back, but later that night when we were sitting on the porch drinking ice cold lemonade, trying to get a breath of cool air while we watched the moonflowers opening and were almost drunk from their perfume, headlights lit up Broadway and Adam pulled up in front of the house in the police car. Osceola and Priddie had gone home and Uncle Josh, sick and tired of all the talk of murder at the dinner table, had gone back to the creek to read so it was just Estella, Mamu, and me. We had the radio on in the house in case there were any news bulletins, but there had been nothing but music, which annoyed Mamu to no end. When Adam turned off the headlights we could see another figure in the car and it was mother. She had been walking from the bus stop when Adam drove by and gave her a lift. For a change, even Mamu, who hadn't said anymore about killing grandfather and was as curious as Estella and me about the murders, was almost happy to see Adam.

"Isn't it just terrible," said mother getting out of the car. "I can't believe it. In Millersburg!" She started up the walk to the porch. "Do you know who the murdered man was? Marius Dorfman. *The* Marius Dorfman. Can you believe that! One of the world's leading tenors killed right here! In Millersburg!"

Adam, for the first time, looked disheveled and unshaven, even sweaty. "Evening, folks. Sure is a hot night, isn't it?" Murder or no murder, Adam was in the habit of giving us the weather report as soon as he got out of the car. "I did hear there might be some rain. That would cool things off a bit. I got your message, Estella."

Mamu gave her a withering look. She didn't know that Estella had called him and she made sure Estella knew that she didn't like it one little bit.

Adam took off his hat and fanned himself. "I've been with state and county police all day."

Estella and I went down the walk to meet him. "Was it really Marius Dorfman?" she asked.

"It sure was. I saw him. Well, what's left of him. The press is going to have a field day with this. Those people are the worst! I never met such rude people in my life. They just don't take no for an answer. They try anything to get in where they're not wanted. Some of them just pushed me aside as though I wasn't even wearing a uniform."

"What do you mean, what's left of him?" My imagination was running wild.

"He was cut up pretty bad."

"Oh, my God," groaned mother. "You mean he was hacked up. Like chopped with an ax?"

"Who was the woman?" I shook hands with him and wondered if he had touched the bodies.

"Gloria Gardiner. Not Mr. Dorfman's wife. Mrs. Claude Gardiner. Big money people. Really big. Their house is up at the east end of the lake. You know the one. With the boathouse built out over the water. Gigantic place. All glass and wood beams and field stone. Right out of a movie. Must have twenty rooms. Like a palace, really it is. Just a beautiful place. I was never in a house like that before."

"Do you know who did it?" Mamu always got right to the point.

"Well, for now it's just speculation. I can't discuss it. You understand, Mrs. Wayland."

"How were they killed?" I wanted all the details.

"Knife."

"Then it wasn't an ax. I heard it was an ax. I would hate to be killed with a knife," said mother. "I can't think of anything worse. Except maybe an ax."

"A knife, an ax . . . what difference does it make? Either way, it's a bad way to get off the carousel." Mamu turned back to Adam, expecting more details.

"Can't imagine any man doing what he did to those people. Gruesome's not the word. Never saw anything like it and hope never to again. Just awful."

"How do you know it was a man who did it?" asked Mamu.

"A woman couldn't do something like that."

"You don't think so?" Mamu smirked.

After the conversation at the breakfast table with the implication that Mamu killed grandfather I thought anything was possible.

"No m'am. It was just awful. Uh uh." He shook his head and repeated. "A woman couldn't do something like that."

"Like what?" He was whetting my appetite.

"It's just not the kind of thing you talk about in mixed company. I'll tell you later, Ben." I was very flattered that Adam and I might have a confidence. One that would exclude Estella.

"Don't be ridiculous. We'll hear about it sooner or later anyway," said Mamu.

"Well, I'm not telling you anything that won't be all over the papers and the radio tomorrow. The woman's throat was slit from ear to ear and . . . and. . . ."

"And what?" Estella wanted to know as much as I did.

"Spit it out, boy," said Mamu.

"I'm not sure I can say this." He looked at Estella and blushed a bit. "In present company, if you know what I mean."

"I'll tell you what you can and cannot say after you've said it. So, say it." Mamu was losing patience.

"And her left breast was cut off." He spit the words out and his face reddened and I'm sure if he could have, he would have gotten back in the car and driven off.

"Oh, my God!" Mother fell into the big wicker chair. "I think I'm going to faint."

"Well, go upstairs and faint," said Mamu, dismissing mother for interrupting Adam when he was getting to the gory parts. "What about the man. The tenor?"

"His private parts were cut off." He couldn't look at anyone when he said it. "Private parts" made him redden even more.

"*Part*," said Mamu, "or *parts*?"

"Parts. The whole works. Everything just cut right off." It was more than he could bear saying and he almost choked on the words.

"Well, I think that should happen to all tenors," said Mamu.

"My God, Mamu. I think you are deranged." Mother was fanning herself with her hands. "Sometimes you just make me sick to my stomach."

"Oh, shut up, Eulalie."

"And," continued Adam, "they were stuffed into his mouth. And his throat was slit. There were some markings cut into his chest, but nobody could figure out what they were."

Mother screamed and fainted dead away, but only after she had heard all that Adam had to say about the disfiguring of Marius Dorfman's corpse.

"Eulalie, stop that foolishness. Ben, throw some lemonade in your mother's face. That girl will do anything for attention."

"I'm not going to throw lemonade in mother's face." Mother's right eye opened just a bit to make sure I really wasn't going to do it.

"Would you like some lemonade, Adam?" Estella was suddenly the perfect hostess and started to pour some for him.

"Thanks, I would." He kept looking at mother, wondering if he should be doing something because every now and then she groaned as if she were in pain.

"Leave her alone. She'll come to eventually." Mamu turned to Adam. "What else?"

"M'am?"

"What else should we know? There were two naked bodies. . . ."

"I didn't say they were naked. I mean they were almost, but their clothes had been cut off them so whoever killed them could mutilate them. Looks like it was some kind of sexual revenge thing. Least that's what Sheriff Anderson says. Well, it would be, wouldn't it?

Parts being cut off like that." He took the glass of lemonade from Estella and tasted it. "Very refreshing. Thank you, Estella. Just the right thing for a hot night like tonight."

I had the most vivid image of the two bodies, lying there in pools of dark, thick blood with pieces of them missing. "Are the bodies still at the house?" I asked.

"Oh, no, they took them to the coroner's office in Laurelwood late this afternoon. The house is all closed up. We've still got a lot of investigating to do."

"Who found the bodies?" Mamu was still after the details.

"Well, now, that's the bad part," said Adam shaking his head. "Really sad. The woman's twelve-year-old son. Says he got up at about three in the morning to go to the bathroom and there they were."

"Where's the husband in all this?" asked Mamu.

"No one knows. Out of town on business, but the boy didn't know where. He travels a lot from what I understand. All over the world, the boy said. His grandparents came from New York and picked him up. Terrible thing for a kid to find his mother like that, isn't it? Can't imagine anything worse, can you?"

"That poor baby," said mother, sitting up straight in the chair. She took Adam's glass and rubbed it on her forehead.

"You OK, Mrs. Whyte?"

"Fine, thank you. It's just that every once in awhile reality makes me black out. What a horrible thing . . . finding your mother all mutilated." She looked at Mamu and there was the slightest hint of a smile.

"Well," said Mamu, getting up, "you finish your lemonade and get back to work, Officer Stoner." The audience was over. "You've got a murderer to catch." She started into the house and without looking at her said to mother, "Eulalie, you'd better get up to bed. All that fainting must have exhausted you." The screen door slammed behind her.

"Thanks for the cold drink," said Adam, gulping down what was left in the glass.

"You don't have to go yet." I thought there might be something that he had forgotten to tell us. And I liked seeing this less-than-perfect Adam.

"Oh, I do. I have to get some sleep. I'm dead on my feet. That is if I can sleep after what I saw today. I guess I have to get used to it. All part of the job. The next few weeks are probably going to be killers. Well, you know what I mean . . . a lot of work. You take care of yourself, Mrs. Whyte. I mean the fainting and all. You might fall and hurt yourself some time."

"Thank you, Adam. You're very considerate. Thank you for the ride home. Estella, walk Adam to his car." I started off the porch. "Ben, you stay here and help me in the house." I knew perfectly well that she didn't need any help; she was just trying to get Estella and Adam alone.

"You need help?" I was annoyed with her.

"Of course I need help. I fainted, didn't I?" She took my hand and pulled herself out of the chair.

"Goodnight, Mrs. Whyte. 'Night, Ben." He and Estella walked down the path to the car and mother and I went into the house.

"You leave the two of them alone, Ben. He's a nice boy. And you know the only reason he comes out here is to see Estella. Does she ever say how she feels about him? I think he's very, very nice, and so good-looking. I bet he's smart. He's always so neat and clean; I like Adam Stoner. Does Estella like him?" Mother had dropped her fragile, slightly stupid act, which she often did when Mamu wasn't around. It was one of the things that infuriated me most about her. Sometime in her life and for whatever reason, she decided that being scattered and shallow was the way to attract attention, so it was the role she chose to play most of the time, but it was as fake as her pearls. She was in reality quite clever and manipulative and very aware of everything that was going on.

"How would I know?" I didn't want to talk about Adam and Estella. "I'm tired. I'm going to bed. Can you make it up the stairs alone?" I said it as sarcastically as I could, but knowing mother, who was intent on matchmaking, she probably missed it. She stood there, lost in thought, undoubtedly planning the wedding.

"I'm fine, thank you. Wait until after he leaves and then bring in the pitcher and glasses. There'll be ants all over the place if you don't. All that sugar. Mamu makes terrible lemonade. I couldn't swallow a bit of it." She was peeking out the screen door trying to see what Adam and Estella were doing. "I just hate ants."

"Let Estella do it." I started up the stairs.

"Ben, what is wrong with you? Is it too much to ask you to bring in a pitcher and some glasses? Good Lord!"

"I said, let Estella do it."

My room was the only bedroom used on the third floor so I managed some degree of privacy. But it was only mine because I slept in it. There was nothing that indicated the personality of the occupant. It was functional and uncluttered, austere as a monk's cell. The way Mamu wanted it. There was little or nothing by way of decoration. One picture hung on the wall over my bed, a scene of an idyllic wood with a shepherd and some fat sheep, all very dark and gloomy and nineteenth-century. I hated it. There was a small cedar chest with treasures I had collected throughout my childhood, neatly packed away so they couldn't be seen. Pebbles I had gathered for some forgotten reason, a butterfly pressed between two small and scratchy pieces of glass, several family photos with my father neatly cut out of all of them, an old medicine bottle that I found sticking out of the clay of the creek bank, a dry snakeskin, and a deck of cards with the king of hearts missing. All things that most seventeen-year-olds would have thrown away but, aside from my clothes, they were the only things in the world that were exclusively mine so I couldn't quite manage to part with them.

In spite of the sparseness I liked the room because it offered sanctuary. No one, except for Mamu, ever entered without knocking. Since I was the only male in the house I was afforded some consideration. In the summer it was the coolest of the bedrooms. With all the windows opened even on the hottest night there was usually a bit of a breeze.

Without turning on the light I took off my clothes and stretched out on the bed. I lay there, staring into the darkness for a few moments before I realized I could hear Estella and Adam talking so I went to the window and watched them. Strained as hard as I could, but I couldn't make out what they were saying, merely a word every so often and an occasional laugh. I remember wondering what they could be laughing about. He had just told us the gory details of two murders and of a boy who found his mother with her throat slit and her breast cut off. "What the hell could they be laughing about?" I thought. Annoyed that I couldn't really hear, I went back to bed and tried to sort out what I was feeling. My brain was too muddled to think clearly and it must have been only a few minutes before I fell asleep. Sleep was infinitely more enticing than trying to sort out my life. Not surprisingly, I had a nightmare about the corpses.

In all my nightmares there were clowns. No demon ever terrified me as much. When Estella and I were little, Mamu and mother took us to New York to the circus at Madison Square Garden. *Ringling Brothers and Barnum and Bailey's Circus. The Greatest Show On Earth.* All the way into the city on the train they kept telling us what a wonderful time we were going to have and Estella and I were beside ourselves with anticipation by the time we got there. It was the first time I had ever been out of Millersburg and I had no idea any place in the world could be so crowded. I didn't like it at all. There were lions and tigers pacing angrily back and forth in circus wagons gaily painted, but incongruously sinister. I felt somehow that we shouldn't be looking at them because I thought they glared at us with a mixture of rage and embarrassment. When we came to the elephants with shackles on their ankles and a huge chain holding them together as they danced back and forth from one foot to the other, I wanted to get away from them because they seemed to be looking at me with their small runny eyes, either accusing or pleading.

"I want to go home," I said.

"Go home! We just got here." Mamu took my hand and pulled me along. "Piffle! I never heard such nonsense."

"I have to go to the bathroom." I didn't, but I wanted to get mother alone, a device I had used as long as I can remember, so I could ask her to take me home.

"Take him to the ladies' room," said Mamu.

"I don't know where it is," whined mother. "How will I be able to find you?"

"There are signs for rest rooms all over the place." She leaned down to Estella. "Do you have to piddle? If so, do it now. We're not coming out once the circus starts."

"I don't have to."

"Come on." Mother took my hand and we started off. "You stay right here by the elephants, Mamu, so we can find you. Oh, I hate this."

"I don't like this place. Can we go home now?" I yelled over the din of all the screaming children.

"Don't be silly, Ben," she laughed. "The circus hasn't even started yet." She dragged me through the crowd. "Don't let go of my hand. If I lose you in this mob I'll never find you again. I don't know what they do with lost boys and girls." I panicked and squeezed her hand as tightly as I could for fear that I'd be lost forever. "Ben, you're hurting me."

"I don't like this place," I repeated. "I want to go home." I knew it was an entreaty that was falling on dead ears and the appeal was hopeless.

"Honey, you are being foolish. Now, Estella is having a good time. Why can't you? Don't ruin it for everyone else. Mamu is getting very angry and we don't want that to happen, do we? We paid good money for the tickets. And once we're inside you are going to love it. All children love the circus. Oh, there's a ladies' room. Come on." She pushed the door open and there were lines of women with children waiting to get in each stall. I could tell by looking at them that some of the kids were as anxious to get away from there as I was.

"Oh, Lord, with all these people we'll be here forever."

"I don't have to go," I said.

"Ben! What is wrong with you? Sometimes you act as though you are seriously troubled. First you have to and now you don't. Which is it?"

"I don't have to. Can we go home?"

"No. We are not going home. That's it. I don't want to hear another word. We're going to have a good time whether you want to or not, damn it! Now come on!" We found Mamu and Estella and went into the arena to find our seats.

"Here we are," said Mamu. "Right in front where we can see everything."

When we were settled I searched the audience, trading glances with several kids in our immediate area who were obviously as scared as me. We were a pathetic brotherhood, a confederacy of the petrified, bonded by fear of the unknown and hoping to get through the afternoon without wetting our pants or worse. I looked up at the rigging, the tightropes and the trapezes and couldn't imagine what was going to happen so high off the ground. I thought I might escape the horror of it all if I kept my eyes squeezed shut, but Mamu saw what I was doing and started scolding me.

"Open your eyes, Ben, and don't be a baby. You're making a fool of yourself. You're such a sissy!"

The three rings were suddenly brilliant with flashing colored spotlights and loud brassy music as the circus parade started around the arena floor. I remember it all in bits and pieces as a person who has witnessed an accident might remember. The wagons with the lions and tigers, furious for being put on display, and the elephants dressed in ballet tutus and Hawaiian grass skirts, looking absolutely mortified. Ponies, decorated with silly feather hats, trudging past with their heads down and dogs dressed in odd little costumes, sailor suits, cowboy outfits, and police uniforms, looking like they were in pain as they bounced along on their hind legs. Men and women in sparkly tights and long capes showing off as they paraded past, and worst of all, there were the clowns. Tall and short, fat and skinny, all dressed in ridiculous clothes with bulbous noses, leering smiles, huge freckles, and painted-on tear drops. I had no idea they were wearing makeup. I thought they were real people, hideously deformed, and I couldn't understand why everyone was cheering for them because they seemed so sad. Suddenly the people in the capes dropped them and started climbing up ropes like spiders and before I knew it they were swinging through the air and others were walking on what looked like strings. There was so much happening, so much to look at, all monstrous and diabolical. To my child's mind it must have been as bizarre as the characters in a Heironymus Bosch painting and I could feel the panic rising in me. I knew I wouldn't be able to stay there much longer. Finally, the clowns drove me screaming from the place. They raced into the audience and I thought they were going to attack us. One came face to face with me, with his wild red hair, blacked out teeth, and cold mean eyes. I got up and raced for the exit with mother, Mamu, and Estella following me. I wasn't the only kid running for his life. There were several with furious adults trailing after them.

When mother caught me she held me by the shoulders and shook me. "What is wrong with you?"

"We're going home. Now," said Mamu, "and we will never ever take you any place again. Do you hear that, Ben? Never." And she walked away, dragging Estella behind her.

"Now, see what you've done," said mother as she followed them, leaving me to tag along in a flood of tears. Just before we left the Garden, Mamu stopped at a vendor's stand and bought a doll for Estella. It was a large clown, as grotesque and menacing as any I had seen running around inside.

"I don't want a doll," said Estella. "I don't, Mamu." She looked at me apologetically as if to tell me the doll wasn't her idea.

"Yes, you do. Now take it." Mamu shoved it into her arms and she reluctantly took it.

No one said anything on the train ride to Laurelwood or the bus ride to Millersburg and nothing was said as we walked from the station to Broadway. Just as we turned into the lane it started to thunder and lightening and we just made it into the house before the rains came. I was immediately taken up to my room. Once I was in bed Mamu came in with the clown doll. I started to feel sick. She pulled the ladder-back chair next to my bed and put the doll on the seat; then she left and turned off the light.

"I don't want to hear a word out of you. Not a word," she said as she closed the door.

It was pitch black and I imagined the clown had gotten off the chair and was walking around in the dark. I thought I heard his big clown feet shuffling along the floor, opening my cedar chest, going through my things. I wanted to tell him to leave them alone. I was terrified. Then there was a flash of lightning and I could see that he was still sitting on the chair staring at me with unblinking and ferocious eyes. I was trapped. Every time the room was washed with the hot, white light and the thunder crashed he seemed to get bigger and bigger until I saw him as a full-grown man sitting next to my bed, leering at me, just waiting for the right moment to do whatever horrible thing he had in mind. I pulled the covers over my head, wondering how I was going to get through the night. When and how I got the courage to do it, I don't know, but somehow I got out of bed, grabbed the doll, ripped the head off, and threw the decapitated monster out the open window into the rain. The last time I ever saw that doll was in a brilliant flash of light, the body lying some ten feet from the head on the wet lawn.

I don't remember anyone ever mentioning the clown again, but I'm sure, when Mamu found the doll, she thought she had taught me a lesson, forcing me to confront my fears. What she didn't know was that when I was tearing the head off the doll I was imagining I was tearing her head off.

The night Adam told us about the murders I dreamt there was only one victim, a clown with a painted smile lying askew like a discarded marionette, in all the gore, with his parts missing. The clown was me. I was also the murderer, dressed in a sequined cape, standing in the middle of Madison Square Garden with a huge, bloody knife in my hand. I was the mutilator and I was the mutilated, the perpetrator and the victim. I awoke in a panic; I don't think I slept the rest of the night.

As I lay there sweating, trying to make some sense out of the dream, trying to figure out who I was, to consolidate the vaporous me, feeling alone and anxious, I had no idea that within one short month, life as we knew it at Broadway Acres would change drastically and that what had taken ten long, impossibly hard years of work and sacrifice, acrimony and, sweat to create would disintegrate and never ever be the same again.

Chapter IV

When my grandfather had disappeared and the dust from the stock market crash finally settled, Mamu discovered there was no money at all. He had been playing with their fortune and thinking he was making a killing, investing every penny they had in what turned out to be worthless stock. The family fortune was gone and the Waylands were ruined. She had never had to deal with money. Even before she married she had what was considered a comfortable life. Her father was a general practitioner in Philadelphia and, although they weren't wealthy by any stretch of the imagination, she grew up in a very comfortable house in a good neighborhood, her mother had a woman in to help, and Mamu never had to think about money. It was always available and she assumed it always would be. And when she married grandfather he saw to that. She said it was the reason she married him. When they met on the beach in Atlantic City in September of 1898 she was not particularly impressed. He was good looking, but he seemed too "full of himself" for Mamu's taste. She was almost thirty and had resigned herself to a life of spinsterhood so she wasn't looking for a man. But her cousin, Alice Pritchard, freckled and glowing, who was engaged to be married and, like many deliriously happy engaged women, felt it was her duty to find men for all her single friends, was determined to find a husband for Mamu. Alice's fiancé, a young and slightly pompous minister in St. Thomas Episcopal Church in Lawneck, New Jersey, a smart and prosperous community just across the Hudson River from New York City, Rev. Thelonius Rigsby, knew Byard Wayland from his army days when he had served as a chaplain. Byard, the war hero, had recently returned from the Philippines. He was vacationing in Atlantic City with some army buddies and quite by accident he and Thelonius ran into each other in the surf. When Alice met him and was informed by the Rev. Rigsby that Byard Wayland was one of *the* Waylands of New York City, "Shipping money, you know," she decided the serendipitous meeting of the two men was the answer to her prayer for Mamu and that the handsome bachelor was the man her cousin was going to marry. Estella and I had heard bits and pieces of the saga from Mamu or Eulalie and even from Uncle Josh, who was only a toddler when they were married, but we were convinced that his contributions to the story were probably the most objective because he often quoted grandfather's version of the story. From what we could remember of our grandfather, an almost invisible figure in our lives even when he lived in the house, he was a no-nonsense man and very grounded, except, we reminded ourselves, when he was playing the stock market. We felt we did know the highlights of their courtship. It was one of those stories a family endures and even relishes telling again and again. How grandfather was quite taken by the energetic and athletic Adela who beat him three times at tennis. Mamu particularly liked telling that part of the story. How he decided the first moment he laid eyes on her that he was going to marry her. She said she should have known right then and there that he didn't have good sense. How he was almost five years her junior and never as long as he lived discovered her true age. When Mamu was telling the story she would pepper it with historical facts that had absolutely nothing to do with her relationship with grandfather. "That was the year the Paris Metro opened, you know." Or, "Bismarck died the same year I met your grandfather. So did Gladstone. And some Italian murdered the Empress of Austria,

Elizabeth. Murdered! Those were omens. I should have known better than to marry him. It all happened too quickly."

By the end of that week in Atlantic City, unimpressed with grandfather, but overwhelmed by the extent of his family fortune and the pressure to get married being applied by cousin Alice, Mamu had decided to accept his proposal when and if he made one. With the help of Alice and the reluctant Rev. Rigsby, an elaborate dinner was planned the Friday before Byard Wayland was to end his leave and return to his army unit, in one of the private rooms of the Breakers Hotel, the most elegant on the boardwalk. Alice searched through Mamu's wardrobe and decided all of her dresses were hopeless because Mamu's tastes were rather plain, and she loaned Mamu one of her own. Mamu liked to tell this part. The dress Alice chose was pale green to show off her eyes and her red hair, and also accentuated Mamu's shoulders which she always thought was one of her best features. It was rather daring, exposing her ample bosom and cleavage, which the Rev. Rigsby couldn't keep his eyes off of and was obviously, at least from what Mamu supposed, promoting sinful thoughts. Alice insisted Mamu wear make-up, something she never did, and perfume applied on all the proper pulse points. By the time she was ready to go to dinner, with a plume fan and a gardenia in her hair, she said she felt like bait. The story was repeated so many times, especially if Mamu had her glass of sherry, that Estella and I could fill in any blanks in case some specifics were overlooked. The table was brilliant with flowers and candlelight, sparkling crystal and silver. The dinner was superb. Coquille Saint-Jacques, Lobster Americaine, Aspèrges étuvées a la crème, and Gateau de Noisette. Mamu still had the small yellowing card on which the menu was printed by an adept calligrapher. They drank champagne with their meal and after coffee Alice and the Rev. Rigsby went for a stroll on the boardwalk, leaving Mamu and grandfather alone. They could hear the orchestra in the ballroom playing "And the Band Played On" while they danced around their little private dining room. He took her out on the terrace, kissed her, and that was it. He proposed.

"I was glad he finally got around to it," Mamu always said at this point in the story, "because I was being eaten alive by mosquitoes and all of a sudden it started to rain and my plumes wilted."

They were married at Christmastime after grandfather was released from the army, at The Little Church Around The Corner in New York. Mamu always interjected that she felt like a hypocrite being married in a church because she didn't believe in God. In fact, she thought it was all too much of a fuss but the wedding was everything her cousin Alice hoped it would be. Estella usually took over at this point in the story because she loved weddings. Mamu wore white and the bridesmaids, including Alice, who was maid of honor, were dressed in red velvet gowns with holly in their hair and in the flower arrangements they carried. "Terrible, prickly bouquets," Mamu always added. There was an enormous Christmas tree left of the altar and garlands of holly and mistletoe were draped everywhere. Mamu said the only thing missing was Santa and his reindeer and someone from the Salvation Army collecting for the needy. The newlyweds honeymooned at Stoneybrook Lodge in the Catskills and both remembered it as one of the worst experiences of their lives. Not, as far as we knew, because they were sexually incompatible. Mamu would never discuss that part of their lives together because if she did it might lead to further discussions of intimacies and her relationship with grandfather. The door was closed on that subject. They saw the new year in "freezing in front of a fireplace that threw no heat whatsoever" and what should have been two weeks of enchantment turned into a test of endurance resulting in frostbite that almost caused permanent damage. Mamu remembered her hands and feet being blue for the rest of the winter.

When they returned to New York they moved into the townhouse on Gramercy Park with his parents, ostensibly until they got settled in a place of their own, while he went to work in his father's shipping firm. Mamu and her mother-in-law declared war the second day they were under the same roof. It started when great-grandmother Wayland discovered that Mamu was a Democrat and she almost had apoplexy. There had never been a Democrat in the Wayland *house,* let alone the family. Catherine Abernathy Wayland was, as Mamu put it, "a witch without a broom." Although she was only in her early fifties she thought of herself as a doyen of New York society. She had had quite a long list of young women she thought were perfect candidates for the prestigious position of her future daughter-in-law, but after one reckless week in Atlantic City, Byard came home and announced he was marrying Adela Pritchard, the daughter of some inconsequential doctor. Worse, a doctor from Philadelphia. No one had ever heard of the Philadelphia Pritchards. She took to her bed for a week and threatened to starve herself to death if he didn't change his mind, but the threat seemed hollow, as Mamu put it, because she was a hefty one hundred pounds overweight and would have lasted six months if not a single morsel of food passed her lips.

Great-grandmother Wayland and Mamu hated each other with a ferocity known only to mothers-in-law and daughters-in-law. Mamu was not about to be molded into the young society matron Catherine had planned on Byard marrying, no matter how hard Catherine tried. And she tried with a vengeance, suggesting clothes to wear, hairstyles, people to see, places to go, and anything else she could think of that she perceived needed her guidance. Mamu accepted none of her suggestions, even if they were sound, because she knew she was driving Catherine mad and so far, that was the most satisfying part of her marriage, she freely admitted. After three months, Catherine, once again, took to her bed, went on a hunger strike, and grandfather decided they should move into the house in Millersburg until they found a place they liked in the city. The country suited Mamu very well, not because she particularly liked it, but because it put enough distance between her and Catherine to make being part of the Wayland family bearable. Mamu soon discovered she was pregnant and they never looked for an apartment in New York. Instead, they settled into Millersburg; grandfather commuted to work every day and slowly and almost imperceptibly they went their separate ways, disappearing into their distinctly private worlds.

At the time, Priddie came in twice a week to clean and do a little cooking, but for the most part Mamu looked after the huge house and the baby. Osceola tidied up the yard and mowed the lawn, but both he and Priddie worked for other people in town, especially in the summer at the height of the season. It wasn't until after the crash, when they lost their jobs because everyone was cutting back, that they spent all their time at the house on Broadway.

When Mamu discovered she was broke she told them she'd have to let them go.

"I don't think Mr. Wayland is coming back. I know he isn't," she said two months after grandfather disappeared. The police, finding no trace of him, had given up the search, convinced that he had assumed another identity and started a new life. "I know this is a bad time for you, but I'm sorry. I'm going to have to let you go. Mr. Wayland's family has told me they wouldn't be responsible for my living expenses. I don't have anything left." She was fishing in her purse to give them their final wages.

"You got the house, ain't you. And you got the land. That's free and clear, ain't it? I mean the bank don't own it." Osceola stood there, staring at Mamu with steady determination. Whatever he had to say he had been thinking about for some time.

"No, the bank doesn't own it. It's free and clear."

"That's more'n most folks got. It's a hell of a lot more'n me and Priddie got, 'scuse my language. We own that little bungalow in Brick Town and hardly enough room in the back to spit. You got twenty-eight acres here. Twenty-eight acres of good land. You can do a lot with twenty-eight acres. Grow a lot of food, you see what I mean?"

"You mean farm it? I don't know anything about farming." She held the few dollar bills out to him, but he wouldn't take it. We were in the kitchen sitting around the table eating lunch and I remember my mother crying. "Eulalie, stop that," snapped Mamu.

"What are we going to do? If Devlin was here he might know." Mother took advantage of every opportunity to remind Mamu of how much better off we'd all be if Mamu hadn't driven my father away. She buried her face in her handkerchief. "We need a man to help us," she mumbled.

"We don't need anybody. Now stop the crying. You're just making things worse," Mamu poked mother in the shoulder. "Pour some milk for the children. Make yourself useful for a change." Mother was too upset to do anything so Priddie got the milk for Estella and me.

"I know about farmin'." Osceola was not about to let a squabble between Mamu and mother keep him from making his point. "I do. I reckon I know all there is to know about farmin'. I don't mean to be blowin' my own horn, but I was raised up on a farm and my daddy was the best I ever knew when it come to farmin'. He never had enough land, but what he did have he turned into bountiful. We never went hungry. You don't have to go hungry neither, Miz Adela."

"But there's no money. None." She looked down at the few dollars in her hand. "This is it."

"All we need is a mule. I can get us a plow for nothin'. I know a man." Osceola always knew "a man," someone who could get him what he wanted or needed. Exactly who these men were we never knew because we rarely saw any of them.

"A mule!" said Mamu with the same shock she would have registered if he had suggested a dragon.

"And we get us some chickens. Priddie can set a hen better'n anybody I ever seen. She got a way with chickens."

Mamu looked at Priddie as though she was expecting some discussion of her expertise with poultry and it was all Osceola needed to see that she was weakening. He also knew she didn't have much choice and that was in his favor. She had absolutely no idea how to get out of her financial predicament.

"We don't know anything about farming," my mother wailed, the tears streaming down her cheeks.

Mamu gave her a withering look. "Eulalie you keep quiet. This has got nothing to do with you." Mother stuffed the handkerchief in her mouth and ran out of the kitchen. We could hear her heavy footsteps on the stairs as she retreated to the safety of her bedroom.

"I'll see to her," said Priddie as she started for the door.

"No you won't. Just leave her alone. She's only trying to get attention. She's been doing that kind of nonsense since she was two years old. We've got more important things than her to think of." She turned to Estella and me. "You want to go upstairs with your mother, then go." We didn't move from the table. I didn't know what Estella was thinking, but I was excited about the prospect of being a farm kid. I had started school the year before and the farmers' children seemed so much older and smarter than the rest of us. And going upstairs to mother presented a problem for me. The problem of allegiance. I was always torn when it came to choosing between my mother and Mamu and Mamu knew it, constantly testing Estella and me. Both of us, either scared or recognizing where the power lay, I never knew which, usually sided with Mamu. When, once again, knowing she had won, she turned back to Osceola and the matter at hand.

"Don't you need feed and hay. . . ?"

"I know a man can help us with that till we're on our feet, you see what I mean?"

"A mule." She thought about it for a moment. "How much is a mule?"

"I can get one cheap as dirt. Course we goin' to need some seed. Just a little money, Miz Adela. Just a little bit. Now's the right time to buy a mule." He was getting excited by the prospect and pressed his point. "It's freezing cold and people ain't got the money to feed their animals. I can get one cheap as dirt. I know I can."

Mamu looked at him for what seemed the longest time and I sat there waiting to see what she was going to say because my future as a farm boy depended on it.

"Wait here," she said and she left the kitchen. Osceola turned to Priddie, who shrugged her shoulders as if to say she had no idea what was happening. Estella kicked me under the table and I kicked her back and she hollered and Priddie scolded us just as Mamu returned.

"Here," She handed Osceola her diamond earrings and engagement ring. "Can you sell these?"

"I reckon I can," he looked at them sparklingly out of place in his rough and callused hand. "But you sure you want to sell 'em?"

"You said you needed money. Well, I don't need diamonds so sell them."

"I won't get what they're worth, you know. Things bein' what they are and all."

"I know that. We need whatever you can get for them. Besides, I won't even know they're gone." Mamu didn't wear jewelry. She didn't approve of it. "If you're going to hang stones around your neck," she'd say, "you might just as well put a bone through your nose or plates in your lips. What's the difference. It's all savage."

"I can get a fine mule. . . ."

"Maybe a cow. What's a farm without a cow?" Mamu went to the window and stood watching the snow falling. She always stared out the window, one hand on her hip, the other unconsciously patting her breastbone, when she was making decisions. "Anyway, we need milk for the children."

"I don't know about the cow."

"Too much money?"

"No, it ain't that. We ain't got any good pasture land."

"And chickens. When do we get the chickens?" There was a light in Mamu's eyes. This was a long shot, but a possible solution to her problems.

"Come springtime. We got to wait till the springtime."

She turned to Osceola who had moved to Priddie's side. "Well, first things first. Sell the diamonds."

"Yes, ma'am. It's gonna work out just fine, Miz Adela. Just fine, you see."

"I don't have any money to pay you. Not now, anyway."

"I know that." He turned to Priddie. "We know that, don't we Priddie?" She shook her head in agreement, obviously anxious to get out of there now that the negotiations were over. "We didn't ask for no money, did we?"

"Why would you do this for me?" asked Mamu.

"We doin' it just as much for us. We ain't got no land. If we did, we be doin' this for ourselfs. We wouldn't need you. But it's different for colored folks. You understand? Though, things bein' as hard as they are, for some folks bein' white ain't goin' to do them a whole hell of a lot a good, is it? White folks starve just the same as colored folks. When times is tough, ain't nothin' the same as it used to be. We got to make new rules. The way I look at it, you need us same as we need you. You can't get along without us and we can't get along without you. You see what I'm sayin'?"

Mamu smiled. She must have appreciated his candor. "Get a good mule or I want my diamonds back."

"Yes, m'am." And they went out through the mud porch.

Mamu turned to Estella and me. "Eat your lunch and stop your gawking." She picked up a dish and started for the sink. "Your mother drives me crazy."

The following weeks were spent getting our new barn in shape. There was such an air of excitement and renewal that even mother joined in, helping whenever Mamu permitted. Estella and I couldn't wait to get home from school every day, racing from the bus stop down Broadway through the snow, to see what progress was being made. Osceola, Priddie, and Uncle Josh worked in the bitter cold, patching the roof and building a stall for the mule that was yet to come, in what had served, in the glory days, as a four-car garage. Most of the lumber used was secondhand that Osceola got from "a man" at a very good price. I never knew how much the diamonds brought, not that it would have meant anything because at that age a dollar was the same as a million, but the money was guarded carefully. What had once been the chauffeur's quarters above the garage became a hayloft.

Space at one end of the main floor was allotted to what would eventually be connected to the hen house. It was obvious that Osceola and Priddie had been planning all this because little time was lost in decision-making. Uncle Josh was a hard worker when he was told exactly what to do and Osceola was very good at letting us all know what he wanted. Mamu gave him carte blanche as long as he worked around grandfather's Cadillac Phaeton, newly sitting on its blocks, pervasive and dusty as a sarcophagus in a Pharaoh's tomb. Over the ensuing years the barn grew around the spectacular car when the odd room was added on here and there as needed. But rather than look like an architectural hodgepodge, I always thought it had certain distinct and obvious utilitarian grace and, from any angle, when silhouetted against the sky, had all the charm of primitive Americana. What made the barn even more special, was that, with each addition, Osceola stood back and looked at it with the satisfaction of a man who, knowing he is getting older, finally watches his dream materialize. Mamu said he was our own Frank Lloyd Wright and true to Mr. Wright's practice of naming his houses: "the Willitts house," "the Coonley house," "the Millard house," Mamu wanted to call it "the Flowers house," but Osceola wouldn't hear of it. "It ain't right . . . seems kinda big-headed." I don't remember who named it, but somehow our splendiferous structure became the Gabarn.

There was no wrangling over the name of our mule when he arrived two weeks after the stall was readied for him. He was already called Sinclair. He was scrawny and hadn't been looked after very well, but contrary to the reputation that proceeded all mules, he was gentle and responded to affection. Mamu thought he was a disaster.

"They should have paid you to take that beast off their hands. That's my money you're playing with, you know. He looks like he's about ready to drop dead."

"When the time comes to start plowin' he'll look like a thoroughbred, Miz Adela. You just wait and see." Osceola patted the mule on the neck. "He's a good old boy, ain't you, Sinclair."

"What a ridiculous name for a jackass. How old is he, anyway?"

"He's just a young fella. About six, the man said."

"More like sixty-six," said Mamu as she threw her hands in the air and walked away in disgust. "I must be out of my mind to go along with this foolishness." She was talking to no one in particular as she slammed the door to the mud porch and went into the house.

"Miz Adela goin' to love this old boy, don't you worry none about that. I just know she is."

It was only a few weeks later when the original Masha, Irina, and Olga arrived.

"I said I wanted a cow." Mamu was much more upset about the goats than she had been about Sinclair when she saw Osceola and Uncle Josh unloading them from the truck.

"I told you, Miz Adela, we ain't got the pasture for a cow. A cow grazes. That means pasture. . . ."

"I know what pasture is. Don't talk to me as though I were an idiot. I'm not a child."

"They're three sisters," said Uncle Josh as he stroked the goats, trying to calm them. "Very unusual for a goat to have triplets."

"It's very unusual for anyone to have triplets." She looked at him as though he was out of his mind.

"I'm just tryin' to explain why I got the goats." Osceola got back on course. "Hold your horses, Miz Adela, OK? Goats don't graze. They browse. We cut way back on feed lettin' 'em browse in the bushes. We can get 'em eatin' the brush when we're clearin' places." Mamu looked at the three nervous goats in disgust. "You said you wanted milk for the children, didn't ya?"

Mamu turned up her nose. "Goats milk is too strong. I don't like the smell and I don't like the taste."

"Did you ever look at a goat's eyes, Adela?" asked Uncle Josh. "Their pupils are unique. Almost oblong."

"I don't give a fig about goat's eyes."

"These ladies," Osceola said pointing to the goats that were unhappily bleating at their new surroundings, "are pure Saanan. What that means is their milk tastes just like Holstein milk. It ain't as much cream as other goats, like the Nubian, but you taste it and you tell me the difference between cow's milk and I give you five dollars."

"You haven't got five dollars."

"Just an expression, that's all."

"And who is going to milk them?"

"I thought the kids maybe and Miz Eulalie . . . and maybe you, Miz Adela."

"I'm not going to milk a goat!" He might just as well have asked her to walk naked down Main Street.

Uncle Josh laughed at the very idea of Mamu squatting next to a goat.

"You see, they got smaller teats than cows. Women's hands are smaller than men and so it's easier for the women and the kids to milk 'em."

The word "teats" startled Mamu and she turned to Estella and me, obviously thinking we shouldn't be listening to such language. "Don't you two have anything better to do than stand there staring like you're feeble-minded?"

"Come on, kids," said Osceola, rescuing us. "Help me get the three sisters into the barn. We fix up a real nice place for 'em." And, as much as they didn't want to go, we led them into their new home. "You goin' to love these ladies, Miz Adela. Just wait and see."

"They're really nice little animals," said Uncle Josh as he helped us. "They have the softest lips."

"I hope you don't expect me to milk a goat!" Mother's voice was tremulous. She had been standing a good distance away in case there was any immediate danger from the strange new beasts.

"Just what are you going to do while the rest of us are working?" asked Mamu folding her arms across her bosom, which was her fighting stance. "If I'm going to learn to milk a goat, then so are you."

Mother gasped at the idea. "I couldn't touch one of them. It would make me sick."

"*You* make me sick," said Mamu.

Estella and I stopped to see what would happen next, but Osceola yanked us into the barn.

"When you two goin' to get smart enough to get out of the line of fire? Lord Almighty, white folks ain't got the brains they was born with."

"Before you go buying camels or elephants, Mr. Osceola Flowers," yelled Mamu, "I want to remind you that I have no more jewels. Whatever money we have from the diamonds is all there is. And I'm not selling the silver. Do you hear me?"

"I didn't ask you to sell the silver, did I?" Osceola stood his ground in the doorway.

"Well I wouldn't put it past you." She turned to mother. "Get in the house, Eulalie. If you're not going to be of any help around here then you'd better think about getting a job." She started down the path.

"A job!" wailed mother. "What kind of a job? I can't do anything."

"Well, neither can Herbert Hoover and he's the president of the United States." She went into the house with mother trailing behind her.

We all stood there watching them go with the goats straining at their tethers and when Mamu was out of earshot Osceola said, "That woman is crazy. What the hell would I want with a goddamn camel?"

The Gabarn and Sinclair and the three sisters were just the beginning of what was to become known in the tri-state area—New Jersey, New York, and Pennsylvania—as "Broadway Acres, Grower Of Superior Vegetables." Osceola and Mamu butted heads every step of the way, both determined to do things the right way which, of course, they thought was their way. More often then not, Osceola was right. Mamu did contribute, however, by controlling his enthusiasm and making sure each new project was completed before the next one was begun. Osceola's plans had a way of tripping over each other and

Mamu did her best to keep them in check. Since she doled out the money things were done if and when she was convinced they were necessary. Fortunately, Osceola was very good at pleading his case and usually got what he wanted. I'm sure they never realized what a good team they were but if they had, neither one would ever have admitted it.

In early spring Osceola brought home a hundred Rhode Island Red chicks. A man owed him a favor so the chicks were free. At least that's what he told Mamu so she couldn't complain about any cash outlay. We set up a brooder in the basement of the house until they were old enough and feathered out enough to go to the hen house. Estella and I looked after them. It was hardly a chore for us because we thought of all the newly arrived livestock as pets. We had never had so much as a dog or cat—Mamu thought they were useless and dirty—and suddenly we were surrounded by creatures that needed our attention. With summer came ducks and guinea fowl and geese. Even Mamu finally surrendered to the animal life. Much to everyone's surprise she did get to like the goats, although she always said they were a bother and more trouble than they were worth. She wouldn't let anyone else milk them once Priddie had shown her how and she was as fastidious about the milking as she was about her housekeeping. Every morning, just before dawn, she scrubbed the pails, took clean hot water to the milking stand, and washed and dried the udders before she started milking. It was all done with the precision of a surgeon. All the while she was at it she talked to them, at first soothingly but eventually, when the goats were used to her and looked forward to being milked, she sat on her little stool, her cheek resting on their hairy side, and while she was milking talked to them as she might talk to old friends. It was a kind of affection and intimacy she was incapable of sharing with another human being. In the beginning she complained about her sore shoulders and back, the shoulders and back of a sixty-year-old woman, she often reminded us, but she enjoyed the three sisters so much that soon it became merely a part of her daily routine. She learned everything she could about keeping goats. There was butter, cheese, yogurt, and ice cream all made under the supervision of Mamu. Her interest in goats became so keen that she even started a correspondence with Mrs. Carl Sandburg, the wife of the poet and biographer, who was an expert in goat husbandry.

Since whatever money there was went into the animals, the land, and anything else that was needed to get the business started, our diet was altered drastically. Mamu was never frivolous when it came to spending money for food and she hated to see anything wasted, but we ate the usual fare. Our meats came from Hampton's Meat Market, our fruits and vegetables from O'Reilley's, and staples from the Millersburg Mercantile. All that changed, except for the occasional trip to the Mercantile for flour and sugar and whatever we couldn't produce ourselves or scavenge. Osceola and Priddie taught us to live off the land and we soon discovered that it was, as Osceola often reminded us, indeed bountiful. We started hunting and fishing for food for the table. Beef and pork were replaced by rabbit and squirrel, chicken by pheasant, woodcock, and quail. And almost every year we had venison. Either Osceola or Uncle Josh got a deer or a friend of Osceola gave us some meat. In the beginning I was too young to go hunting, but I did help with the traps. We trapped muskrat along the banks of Settlers Creek for the pelts, and when Priddie said we were going to eat the meat I thought my mother would faint dead away.

"I am not going to eat a rat!" She turned to Mamu. "God, mother, is there no end to this?"

I wasn't too keen on the idea of eating a rat myself.

"It's better'n chicken," said Osceola. "You eat squirrel, don't you? It's a rodent just like Mr. Muskrat. So's Mr. Rabbit. I don't notice you turnin' your nose up when Priddie puts a good rabbit stew on the table."

"I know, but. . . ." I started to protest.

"You skin 'em, don't you, boy? If you can skin 'em you can eat 'em." I was as good at skinning the game as Osceola and Uncle Josh.

"I am going to be sick. I swear, every day around here is more like living in an insane asylum," said mother as she fled to the security of her bedroom.

"I think it will be a lot easier to swallow if you don't refer to them as Mr. Muskrat and Mr. Rabbit. It gets a little personal, even for me," said Uncle Josh.

"I see what you're sayin'." Osceola started to laugh.

"The meat's very nice. And they're much bigger than a barn rat. Just forget the rat part of their name. That's what's botherin' you. They ain't nothin' like a rat." It was hard not to believe whatever Priddie said. "Just like a rabbit, those little animals are vegetarian. They are as clean as can be. Livin' in the water all the time. Compared to a chicken, which will eat anything . . . includin' another chicken . . . the muskrat is a very decent animal." Decent was a word that meant a lot to Priddie. "The meat is light and sweet. I think you'll like it fine. Try it. That's all I'm askin' you. OK?"

That night Priddie served the first muskrat we ever ate. She stuffed them just as she did poultry and when she put the platter on the kitchen table, smelling deliciously of cooked onions and sage and garlic, the perfectly browned carcasses surrounded by glazed carrots, potatoes, and parsnips, any objection I had to eating them started to fade quickly. Mother refused to come to the table and was sitting out the new gastronomic experience in her room. We all sat staring at them for several moments, not knowing quite how to attack them. Even Estella and Uncle Josh, who were ready for any adventure, seemed hesitant. It was Mamu, who finally reached out and cut off a hind leg, who broke the silence.

"They smell delicious, Priddie. They really do." She looked around the table. "Well, what are you waiting for? Pass me your plates. Ben?"

It *was* delicious and my favorite of all the game we ate. Osceola was right; it was better than chicken.

When spring arrived we moved into the next phase of living off the land and our teacher was Priddie. We gathered the tender young "fiddles" of the fiddlehead fern, which Osceola likened to asparagus only better, dug cattail roots, and picked May apples from under their little green umbrellas. On the banks of several streams running off Settlers Creek there were patches of wonderful, peppery watercress. Priddie transplanted some to a wet spot under a faucet we couldn't get to turn off completely on the side of the house and we had cress all summer just outside the door. We picked mushrooms from their fairy rings, which she said could only be done in the very early morning because the fairies were lazy and slept late and wouldn't catch us stealing from them. Estella and I knew there were no fairies, of course, but pretending there were made the gathering that much more fun. And Priddie did everything she could to make our work fun. She knew what hard work lay ahead for us. There were dandelion greens and purslane and if Priddie couldn't find anything else she steamed young violet leaves, which, she said, when eaten regularly, warded off cancer. "That's what my Auntie Moll say and she knows everything about everything." It was just one of hundreds of her natural cures. Sweet potatoes for diseases of the blood, elder flower and mint to break a fever, lemon balm to induce sleep, rose hips to fend off colds, yarrow to stop bleeding and for "women's troubles" and garlic for almost any other ailment. "And don't forget parsley. Ain't nothing better for the nerves and it looks good and it tastes good, too. And butterflies lay their eggs on the parsley. Eggs not half the size of a grain of rice. Yes, they do." The woods and fields and creek were a veritable pharmacopoeia to her and she gathered herbs, dried them, and kept them in the pantry in mysterious, odd little jars with no labels. She knew them all by sight, touch, and smell. We learned so much from her and at the same time we learned about her. Until she and Osceola became permanent fixtures at the house she was merely a little woman who came in to clean occasionally. She did what was expected of her and moved on to her next employer. There was no territorial imperative. But when she was there every day from sunup to sundown and made the kitchen and garden her own, we had the opportunity to see how incredibly knowledgeable she was. She couldn't read or write, but seemingly there was nothing she didn't know and consequently Estella and I drove her crazy with questions. Very rarely did she tell us she was too busy and send us on our way.

When the wild berries came into season we had blackberries, raspberries, strawberries, and huckleberries. Then Priddie made pies, pancakes, muffins, and preserves which we had all through the winter.

One day Osceola announced that we were going to have to start finding days when we could go to the shore. At the time, the very idea of going to the ocean seemed as remote as going on a trip to Uncle Josh's Tassili Mountains.

"I ain't sayin' there's anything wrong with the fish from the creek and the lake, but there's a whole ocean there just waitin' to give us all kinds of good stuff. I'm gettin' kind of tired of eel. Ain't you? And not just the ocean. You got the Barneget Bay, too. I caught a flounder there one time bigger'n the whale that ate Jonah. And crabs. Umm umm. God amighty! We catch us a mess a crabs and take 'em home and throw 'em in a pot. Now, that's good eatin'."

Mamu wasn't convinced that our taking trips to the shore was such a good idea, but as usual Osceola worked his magic and we started going about once a month. We always went on Sunday because Priddie wouldn't work, except for looking after the animals, on the Lord's day and Osceola, whose homage to the Lord came and went at his convenience, took advantage of her piety to have some time to do things he either wanted to do for pure pleasure or couldn't get to during the week. Mamu and Eulalie looked after the stand. Sundays were the only times Mamu worked the stand and that was because we were putting food on the table. Religion was not an issue for her because she didn't practice any. Priests, ministers, and rabbis were all charlatans as far as she was concerned, in the same category with lawyers and doctors. Even though her father had been a doctor, she didn't trust any of them. I don't think she trusted anyone. Mamu's misanthropy was flat-out across the board.

Estella and I, and occasionally Uncle Josh, would pile into the truck before dawn and head for whatever destination Osceola had decided on. Brielle, where the Manasquan river emptied into the ocean, because he knew a man who had a boat there, Mantoloking, on the slip of land between the ocean and the bay, because there was a man who gave him bait, and Lavalette just because a one-eyed man who owed him money lived there. To us the names of the towns were right out of the *Arabian Nights*. Millersburg was less than forty miles from the ocean, but before we started making our monthly Sunday jaunts Estella and I had only been to the shore once. That was before grandfather disappeared when the whole family, to show off his new Cadillac Phaeton, went for a leisurely drive to Deal, the most exclusive seaside resort in New Jersey, to see friends of his whom Mamu hated. Mother was carsick all the way there and back and Mamu, who had recently gotten her driver's license and was angry because grandfather wouldn't let her drive, screamed at her the whole time not to throw up in the new car. I always associated that short trip with the ocean and never wanted to go again. But all that changed with our excursions.

It took about an hour to get to the shore but in that short time the landscape changed dramatically from the rich brown of home to an even richer red where the terrain flattened and the tall trees started to disappear, replaced by pines and scrub. By the time we got to the shore the soil had faded and mellowed to the soft beige of the sand. Without the tall trees to obstruct our view, the horizon started to slowly but noticeably expand, and as we got closer, almost palpably, the air changed. I don't know if Estella, Osceola, and Uncle Josh reacted as strongly as I did, but the taste of the salty air nourished some primordial part of me and I always started to feel something I never felt anywhere else. It was a strange mix of emotions, loneliness, insignificance, and, at the same time, a sense of renewal. And there was something more pervasive, something I couldn't bring into focus. I wasn't sure what the feeling was until years later when I stood on the craggy coast of Maine looking at the ocean on a crisp autumn day and realized that what I always sensed was some kind of immortality. There it was, shimmering in the vastness and timelessness of infinity. There was no end to it and when I was there I felt there was no end to me. I would always be a part of the dunes with the sea oats rattling and the gulls crying as they sailed overhead on the wind currents while the sand crabs busily skittered sideways as they had done for a million years. The heady smells, the blend of brine, sea creatures, kelp, and fragrances blown in from unknown and unimaginable places would only intoxicate if I was there to appreciate them. The sandpipers, intense and precise as they danced along the edge of each incoming wave looking for food, did it for me too. I felt I would be a part of every sunset and sunrise, every cloud and every storm because I was a part of something that would never end. It was the promise of immortality and it was so seductive and inviting that I never wanted to go home at the end of the day. I could easily have become one of those people who happily, if compulsively, give up everything, including their life, for the sea.

In the summer we went crabbing and clamming in the bay. We rowed out to wherever Osceola felt in his bones that the crabs were waiting for us, dropped our crab traps off the boat, and lazed in the sun eating egg salad sandwiches and drinking iced tea that Priddie had prepared for us. On a good day we could fill a bushel basket with the bug-eyed, blue-legged critters. Osceola was very careful to throw back any that he considered too small. "We be back to get you next year," he'd say. Or, "You one lucky, ugly crab. We goin' to let you go this time." When we went clamming, we walked into the bay pulling an old patched inner tube with a burlap bag tied inside and when we felt the clams with our toes we went underwater and dug them out with our fingers, dropping them into the bag. Nothing else that we did in our quest for food was quite so exquisitely and wonderfully exhausting. We took more clams than we could ever use but they never went to waste. On our way home at the end of the day we'd stop at the First Baptist Church of the Nazarene in Brick Town and the pastor, Rev. Hector Motherwell Box, who was one of the thinnest men I had ever seen, with a space between his teeth so wide that another tooth could have fit, would take whatever Osceola had to offer and distribute it to his congregation as needed. We'd also stop by the Flowers' house. Those were the only times we ever saw the mystery woman who looked after the peculiar Camille. She was pretty, coffee-colored, and always wore a lot of jewelry and bright colored dresses. She never came out to the truck and we never went inside. She'd wave at us and smile, but when Osceola gave her whatever he was delivering she disappeared into the house and we went on home. When we'd ask about her, Osceola would dismiss our questions with, "She's just a woman, that's all." It was very strange to think that Priddie and Osceola, who spent so much time with us, had another life. A life we knew nothing about and a life that I somehow knew would never, under any circumstance, include us. They were black and we were white. They knew everything about us and we knew only what they'd cautiously allow about them. Theirs was a secret society.

We also fished for flounder in the bay. At times, if the water was shallow enough, we could see them scooting along the bottom, flat as pancakes. We caught weakfish, which were sea bass with jaws so weak that the hook would pull out, and sea robins which made a weird little noise, somewhere between a croak and a bird chirp, had wings, and were what Osceola called "trash fish." Estella's favorites were the blowfish, which we always threw back after Osceola had tickled them and they blew up like balloons.

The boat he borrowed belonged to a man in Brielle, Eddie Ninetoes.

"He lost his little toe to a snappin' turtle when he was just a kid. Bit it clear off his foot. Bone and all. Nice fellow, Eddie. Born in Harlem. Old Eddie also got the biggest dingus on the East Coast. Least that's what I heard tell. But he only got one ball. Funny the way things work out, ain't it? I guess you got to give a little to get a little, you see what I mean? 'Cept in his case he give a little and got a lot. The Lord works in funny ways, don't He though? If you ask him he'll show you where the little toe is missin'. I ain't sure if he'll show you his dingus or not. Don't expect so."

We never asked to see his dingus, but he was very accommodating when we asked to see where the missing digit had been.

"That devil bit right through my old shoe and took my toe. He was so big I though his head was his shell." Eddie Ninetoes was a huge man with a shaved head and no matter what he said, he smiled. "I hope somebody got the bastard and made soup out of him. Mean son-of-a-bitch." All the time he was telling the story Estella and I stared at his crotch, hoping to catch some hint of his other deformity.

In those years right after the crash there was one other search that went on of a Sunday afternoon that had nothing to do with food or, if it did, it was only coincidental. When Priddie and Osceola started working full-time our flower garden consisted of a few rose bushes and some tiger lilies, but by the time Broadway Acres was a going concern our flowers were as impressive as the vegetables and our stock was free, taken from derelict and deserted homesteads and farms. Osceola and Priddie, armed with buckets and bags and a shovel, would drive down country roads and "rescue" plants that had been left behind by people who either had lost their land or had moved on to what they thought would be a better life. Estella and I never went with them because Mamu said it was their private time. Had we asked to go along I'm sure they would have included us but, because they never invited us, we knew that those Sundays were theirs to spend together. There was no end to the selection of plants they found. Peonies and iris of every color, asters, chrysanthemums, wisteria and roses, lilac and mock orange, lily-of-the-valley and daffodil. What Priddie admired most about the flowers and bushes she gathered, aside from their potential beauty, was their strength. "These be survivors," she said, "survivin' is what it's all about. The survivors make very good stock." I knew she wasn't just talking about plants. In just a few years, when our gardens were in full bloom, with Priddie's innate and unerring sense of color and form, they may not have rivaled Giverny, but had she the resources she would have given Monet a run for his money.

Chapter V

It was just under a year from the time we started building the place when mother got the job at Schiller's lumberyard in Laurelwood. She had been reading the few employment ads in the paper, but since she had no experience there were none that she felt she could apply for. The ad for the lumberyard said, "no experience necessary" and "apply in person" and when she told Mamu that she was going to apply for the job it instigated a horrendous fight.

"I need bus fare to Laurelwood."

"It's a waste of money."

"You're the one who said I should get a job."

"You won't get a job."

Mother was on the verge of tears. "Just once, just once," she said it louder the second time, "I wish you'd be on my side. Have I ever in my life done anything right? Anything to please you? Tell me."

"Nothing comes to mind. I'll have to think about that." Her arms folded across her bosom.

"I wish I could go away from here. I really, really wish I could go so far that I'd never have to come back."

"Go. I'm not stopping you."

"I can't. I have the children."

Mamu's eyes narrowed. "They don't need you." She turned to us. "You don't need your mother, do you? What does she do for you?" I didn't know what to say and Estella started crying.

"You are a vicious woman, mother. How can you be so cruel? How can you say that to my children?"

Priddie took us by the hand. "Come on, kids, I got somethin' to show you outside." And she took us to the Gabarn.

"I can hear 'em all the way out here," said Osceola, who was cleaning Sinclair's stall.

We could hear them screaming at each other for the next several minutes until mother came out the back door folding money and putting it in her purse. She started down Broadway.

"You need a ride Miz Eulalie?" called Osceola.

"No. I want to walk, thank you." She started running, her ankles occasionally twisting in the ruts in the road.

"Why don't they just kill each other and get it over with?" he said, almost to himself.

"You mind what you sayin'!" scolded Priddie.

That night, mother came home and timidly announced that she was employed.

"I got the job at Schiller's, Mother."

Mamu, who was folding laundry with Priddie, refused to turn and look at her. "Doing what, may I ask?"

"Looking after the office. Schiller's lumber yard."

For a moment, Mamu didn't say anything. "You're late for supper."

"I don't want anything." There was an almost imperceptible strength in my mother's voice.

"I fix you something, Miz Eulalie. . . ."

"She said she didn't want anything!" Mamu glared at Priddie.

"Thank you, Priddie. Really, I'm not hungry. I think I'll just go up and take a bath."

"Congratulations." Priddie almost whispered it.

"Thank you very much." She kissed Priddie on the cheek and started out of the room. Priddie stood there in shock because there was never any display of affection in our house. Not to anyone.

"When do you start?" Mamu still hadn't turned to her.

"Tomorrow."

"And what are you going to do for bus fare?"

"My new employer, Mr. Cowles, gave me an advance. But thank you, mother, for your concern." There was a definite edge to her voice and Mamu stiffened. Mother left the kitchen and went upstairs. It was only a minor skirmish, but to her it was a major battle and she had won.

That tiny bit of independence must have enraged Mamu because she stood frozen at the laundry basket, not knowing what to do next.

"I thought you two were going to catch night crawlers with Uncle Josh," she finally said.

"Go on. They out back waitin' for you. It's dark enough now." Priddie pushed us out the door. "Miz Adela, you be nice to Miz Eulalie. . . ." we heard her say as she went back into the kitchen. "She tryin' her best."

The barn swallows were making the last of their swipes for insects before it got too dark, when the bats would take over. We could see the silhouettes of Osceola and Uncle Josh who were standing in the back yard talking. It was a perfect evening for catching night crawlers, which were our preferred bait. It had rained that afternoon and the soil was soft enough for the big worms to push through with little effort. All we had to do was pick them up and drop them in a can.

"Mama's got a job," yelled Estella and she started to dance around as if the news needed more than the telling. Uncle Josh turned on the flashlight and Estella's shadow appeared on the blank back wall of the house.

"A job! That's good. That's real good," said Osceola. "Miz Eulalie got a job. I never thought that would happen. Not in a million years. Good for her."

"Estella, walk toward me and watch your shadow." She did and her shadow got bigger and bigger. "The further you get away from the house the bigger your shadow gets." Mother appeared in the upstairs bathroom window and started laughing as Estella danced back and forth, changing the size of her shadow.

"Hey, Miz Eulalie, good for you."

"Thank you, Osceola. Thank you very much. I start tomorrow. I'm a working woman. How do you like that?"

"That's wonderful, Eulalie. Really it is." Uncle Josh shone the flashlight on her. "You're in the spotlight."

Mother giggled, disappeared from the window, and a few moments later we could hear loud music, an orchestra playing swing. Mamu, followed by Priddie, came storming out the back door.

"What's that racket?" The music was coming from the bathroom window.

"It's music, Mamu," shouted mother. "You know what music is, don't you?" Mamu was not a music lover. It was just a lot of noise as far as she was concerned and when mother wanted to listen to the opera being broadcast from the Metropolitan Opera House on Saturdays Mamu said she'd rather listen to a chicken fight than all that screeching.

"Dance, Estella," called Uncle Josh. "We're shadow dancing, Adela. Come on."

"Dance, honey," called mother. "You're a good dancer."

"Wait a minute. Wait just one little minute, I got a idea," and Osceola ran around the side of the house.

"Come on, Ben. Dance." Estella was spinning around, going closer to the flashlight and then back toward the house.

"You're in Turkey, you're a whirling dervish," said Uncle Josh as she spun faster and faster.

I couldn't resist and started dancing to the music too, making my shadow do all kinds of contorted things. Even Priddie, in her gentle way, couldn't stand still and joined in. We could see mother in the bathroom window and could hear her laughing.

"Okay," called Uncle Josh, "now you're in Australia . . . you're an aborigine. Let's see your aborigine dance." Estella started stamping her feet and I followed her lead.

"Stop it this minute." Mamu looked up at the window. "Eulalie, turn that radio off. Good Lord, they'll be able to hear that in downtown Millersburg."

Just then Osceola came around the corner in the truck and parked it so the headlights lit up the back of the house.

"That's great," said Uncle Josh as he turned off his flashlight and joined in the dancing. "Okay, now we'll do a rain dance."

Osceola, apparently too reserved to dance, started making shadow animals. "Come on, Miz Adela, join in the fun."

Mamu stood, feet apart, staring at us as though she was witnessing the fall of Gomorrah. "I've never seen such foolishness. Stop it this minute."

"Adela," Uncle Josh said,, jumping up and down, doing his version of a rain dance, "come on, help us. We need all the rain we can get."

"It rained all day. What is wrong with you?"

Uncle Josh and mother started laughing uncontrollably and Mamu was ready to kill the lot of us.

We were all dancing, Priddie and Estella and Uncle Josh and I, even Osceola started to sway back and forth. We were completely lost in the music, spinning, jumping, racing back and forth increasing and decreasing the size of our shadows. Mamu kept shouting at us to stop, but we didn't pay any attention to her. It was a glorious moment of rebellion. Mother's fleeting show of independence had somehow galvanized us. There was a kind of madness that took over and for once we weren't afraid of Mamu. She was standing right there watching and admonishing us and we paid no attention to her as we danced and danced. But I clearly remember that none of us ever touched. Our shadows looked as though they were dancing together, but it was merely illusion because there was never any contact. Not so much as a hand being held. Some barriers just couldn't be broken no matter how intoxicating the situation. Mamu finally gave up and went back into the house, and a few minutes later the music stopped and so did the frenzy. The moment had passed, the dance was over, and we stood, our shadows as frozen as we were, trapped in the harsh glare of the headlights like frightened deer.

Mamu had won again as she would win over and over for the next ten years until that steamy summer when the world was plunged into war, I turned seventeen, and the two strangers were slaughtered at the lake.

Chapter VI

The world was shocked and saddened by the news of Marius Dorfman's death. It said so right on the front page of the *Daily Reminder*. His name was in the headline but Gloria Gardiner's picture was as big as his was. Hers was demure, the obviously well-bred young society matron, every blond hair perfectly in place, lips well-defined, eyes, large, soft, and slightly dreamy. His was one of his publicity shots, theatrical and slick with him holding a cigarette and wearing a cravat with a casual, open-collared shirt. They were a very handsome couple. Almost every radio station was alternating between news of the murders and playing bits of his recordings of famous arias. Mamu cringed every time they did and changed the dial looking for non-musical news. Her favorite, Mr. Gambling, was reminding us that although the ghastly discovery in Millersburg was indeed shocking, we weren't to forget that things in Europe were about to boil over.

"I think I'm going to take piano lessons. Everyone should be able to play at least one piece of Mozart in their lifetime." Uncle Josh breezed into the kitchen to join us for breakfast, something he rarely did because he preferred to have his coffee at creekside without having to listen to the radio. He contended that news, good or bad, first thing in the morning was unnatural, unhealthy, and very bad for the digestion. "Can I practice on the piano in the sitting room, Adela? We'll probably have to have it tuned."

"Piano lessons at your age! Don't be ridiculous. And hush up. I'm trying to listen to the radio. That Hitler is up to no good." She turned the radio louder so she wouldn't have to listen to Uncle Josh's nonsense.

"Mornin' Mr. Josh. It's nice to see you up here for a change." Priddie was very fond of him and whenever he came into her kitchen there was a marked change in her mood. "You like some bacon and eggs?" she asked as she poured him a cup of coffee.

"Perfect."

"I think you should take the piano lessons." She went to the icebox and took out the eggs and bacon. "Be nice to have that old piano gettin' some use. I wouldn't mind dustin' it if somebody played it once in awhile. Don't you think so, Miz Adela?" She winked at us because she knew how much music annoyed Mamu.

"I said, hush. I'm trying to listen to the radio."

"Adam Stoner was here last night." I wanted to tell Uncle Josh all the details of the murders.

"He told us all about the people who were cut up." Estella jumped in ahead of me. "Their pictures are on the front page." She shuffled through the papers looking for the news section.

"Now don't go tellin' us all that ugly stuff again. Good Lord, the man ain't even had his breakfast." Priddie turned to Uncle Josh. "That's all they been talkin' about all mornin'."

"One of the dead people is Marius Dorfman," said Estella.

Uncle Josh, who was about to put sugar in his coffee, froze. "Marius Dorfman," he repeated almost inaudibly. "Oh, Jesus!"

"And the woman was named Gloria Gardiner." I said it quickly before Estella had the chance. "Her left breast. . . ."

"Oh, Jesus Christ." He dropped the spoon, spilling sugar all over the table. Estella handed him the paper. He took one glance and the color drained from his face. He squeezed his eyes shut, making almost indistinguishable garbled sounds that ended in a clear and resonant "Fuck!"

"You watch your language," said Mamu, "or you get out of this house."

"You all right, Mr. Josh?" Priddie went to him. None of us had ever heard him swear or use a bad word before, but seeing how obviously upset he was, Priddie overlooked the transgression. "You look like you goin' to fall over."

"I don't want any breakfast." He dropped the paper, pushed the chair back from the table, and got to his feet. "I . . . I . . . please. . . ." He turned and ran out of the kitchen, and I followed. I could hear Mamu calling after me to finish my breakfast and telling Estella to sit right where she was. I stayed close to him as he raced past the Gabarn and onto the path through the woods to his shack. Halfway to the creek he stopped and started retching, but since there was nothing in his stomach he just heaved convulsively for a few minutes.

"Uncle Josh. . . ."

"Please Ben, leave me alone. Just go back to the house and leave me alone." He started convulsing again.

"But you're sick. Let me help."

"I'll be all right. Just go back. . . ."

"I can't leave you like this."

"Goddamn it, Ben, leave me alone." I had never seen such pain and rage in a face. "Get out of here. Just go. Go!" His eyes welled up with tears. "Please, Ben, go away." He continued along the path, but I didn't follow. When he was out of sight I went back to the house.

Mamu was annoyed. "I never saw him act that crazy. And I never ever heard him use language like that. You tell me what was wrong?"

"I don't know. He didn't say."

"All that killin' talk! That's enough to upset anybody. No wonder the poor man didn't want no breakfast."

"Well, I suppose we won't be seeing him in the fields today. Ben, you and Estella help the Hungarian boys."

"Who's going to look after the stand?" asked Estella.

"Priddie can do it."

"No, I can't. I'm makin' catsup today and I already squished the tomatoes."

"Then I'll do it. Why is everything so difficult?" Mamu grabbed her apron and went out the back door.

At lunchtime Priddie fixed a tray for Uncle Josh and I took it down to the shack. We had to do it without Mamu knowing because she was furious with him and wouldn't have approved of, what she would have called, coddling. I had never in all the years he lived there knocked on his door because I always felt free to just walk in. But that day, for whatever reason, I knocked and there was no answer.

"Uncle Josh," I called after knocking several times, "are you in there?" Still there was no answer. "Priddie made you a sandwich." I started to feel cold because my mind was right on the edge of jumping to horrible conclusions.

"I'm here, Ben." His voice came from behind me and I turned and saw him sitting in the rowboat which was tied to the dock, riding the current about ten feet out.

"Priddie made you lunch. What are you doing?" I walked along the dock and stood looking at him with the tray in my hands, not quite knowing what to do.

"I'm not hungry." He made no move to pull the boat closer to the dock.

"You have to eat something." I put the tray down and sat with my feet dangling over the creek. "You going to tell me what's wrong? Please. You can trust me. I won't say anything, I swear. I'm sorry I talked about the murders when you were going to eat your breakfast. . . ."

"Oh, God, that wasn't it," he interrupted. "It wasn't your fault." He looked at me for what seemed like a full minute before deciding to go on. "I knew her." He didn't say anything else, he just sat there staring at me, the sun dancing through the willows on his tortured face.

I didn't know what to say so finally I just said I was sorry.

"I knew her, Ben," he repeated. "I met her when I was at Princeton at a house party weekend. She was Gloria Fulton then. She went to Vassar. That was long before she married Claude Gardiner. So long ago. Oh, Jesus." He took in a deep breath and looked away. "I want to be alone. I hope you understand."

"Yes, I do." I did and I didn't. I understood that we didn't share our feelings, talk about what was bothering us or, in adversity, look for support from one another. That was the rule. But what I didn't understand, in the face of so much agony, was why there couldn't be an exception to the rule. So I said it. "No, I don't understand. Why do you want to be alone when you're so miserable?"

"Because I have to think. I need time alone to think. I don't know what to do."

"Why do you have to do anything?"

"Please, Ben, if you want to help just go away and leave me to myself."

There was nothing to say so I left the tray on the dock and went to work in the fields with Estella and the boys.

"How is he?" she asked.

"The same. He doesn't want to talk about it."

"Maybe he'd talk to me."

"I don't think so. He said he wants to be alone to think." That's all I told her because I didn't want to talk about it either. Estella took her basket and moved to another row of tomatoes and I was left to my thoughts. All I could think of was a young Uncle Josh at a house party weekend at Princeton. I never before thought of him in his college days. I never thought of him in any context that wasn't a part of our lives in Millersburg or in some incredibly romantic and adventurous place out of one of his fantasies: the Trans-Siberian Railroad, an island, a mountain, or a jungle he had pinpointed on one of his maps. And, even more surprising to me that day, as I picked the tomatoes, listening to Stash and Janos talking and laughing as they chatted on in Hungarian, I had never thought of him in any kind of relationship with a woman. Or even with a friend. As far as I knew, he saw no one but the family and Priddie and Osceola. We were all a part of the very small world in which we lived and no outsider ever moved in.

That evening we celebrated my birthday. Priddie fussed a good deal and made all my favorite dishes, so despite the tension it managed to be rather festive. During dinner, there was a vague reference to attending the World's Fair. I think it was Estella who brought it up.

"Maybe when the weather cools." Mamu used the heat as an excuse for getting out of doing everything she didn't really want to do. Not that she felt she needed an excuse.

"The king and queen of England didn't mind the weather. They went to the fair." Estella really wanted to go as much as I did so she was pressing hard.

"Well, Ben's not the king of England and you're not the queen. I said, we'll see. Right now it's too hot to think about anything. Let's have the cake on the porch, there might be a breeze. We won't wait for your mother. Who knows when she'll be home? And I think your uncle has finally gone completely crazy so we won't even think about him." Before anyone could agree or disagree, Mamu got up from the table and went outside. Priddie and Estella served the cake and coffee on the porch and Osceola brought out my presents, all wrapped, I was sure by Priddie, in colorful remnants of cloth from Mamu's sewing room. I opened the largest one first.

"I hope you like the color," said Osceola.

"That's his way of telling you he did the shopping." Mamu rocked in the chair without looking at me.

There was a blue plaid flannel shirt and under it a pair of dark brown corduroy trousers.

"That's the color blue you like, ain't it?" asked Osceola.

"Yeah. It's a great shirt. And I like the pants, too."

"Granted," said Mamu, "it's a little warm to think about wearing corduroy and flannel now, but they'll be nice for school." She still sat there staring straight ahead. Just a few weeks earlier she had told me there was no reason for me to go back to school. But somehow Osceola got to her and it was her way of saying she had changed her mind.

"You really like 'em?" asked Osceola. He winked at me and nodded his head.

"Open mine next." Estella handed me a small box and when I opened it there were three pair of underpants.

"Underwear! How come you bought me underwear?"

"Priddie said you needed it. Blame her."

"Well, you do. There ain't nothin' left to mend in the underwear you got. And if you don't like that, you ain't goin' to like what Osceola and me got for you. Handkerchiefs. You need them, too. So there."

There was one small box I hadn't opened.

"This is from Miz Eulalie. She said make certain you open it with your other presents."

It was a cat's eye ring. I was shocked when I saw it because it was such a frivolous gift for anyone in our family to give. Even though times had gotten so much better we all lived with a Depression-era mentality.

"I already saw it," said Estella. "It's beautiful, isn't it. Put it on. I told Mama it would fit. She thought it might be too big."

I slipped it on the ring finger of my left hand, admiring the way the gold looked against my tanned skin.

"That must have cost a pretty penny," said Mamu. "Where'd she get the money for that?" She leaned in for a closer examination. "It's nice on your hand." She turned away and looked up at the moon, which was just beginning to show. I couldn't believe how pleasant she was being and I suspected that she had taken a detour to the sherry on her way to the porch.

The cat's eye ring is the only piece of jewelry I have ever owned, aside from a watch, and to this day I wear it. Age and arthritis have thickened my fingers and I now wear it on my little finger, but all

I have to do is look at it, even though time has diminished the bit of fire in the eye, and every detail of that particular birthday comes flooding back. It was the last birthday I would spend at home.

Conversation lagged after the gifts and the cake and coffee, so Osceola, in an effort to keep the evening light, started talking about Sinclair, who by then was semi-retired as a plow mule because of the much more efficient tractor, but was still expecting to go to work every morning.

"Just like a human person, that mule just don't want to retire. My daddy always said retirement killed more men than all the wars put together. Well, that's one disease most colored folk ain't got to worry about. The retirement disease, I mean." He waited for someone to comment but no one did. "I still hitch Sinclair up every once in a while just to make him feel good, you know what I mean? I guess a mule's got to think he's earnin' his keep, too."

No one was particularly interested in Sinclair's state of mind in spite of the fact that after ten years he was a beloved member of the family. The disturbing behavior of Uncle Josh when he discovered the identity of the murder victims was all anyone could think of even though no one was talking about it. Osceola moved on to the goats, thinking it might spark some conversation, especially with Mamu.

"Irina be comin' in season soon. I'll take her to the buck soon as she does."

"I'll take her," I said. I jumped at the chance to drive by myself because it was the greatest freedom I knew.

"You be a legal driver now," said Osceola with false enthusiasm. "You be a drivin' man, that's for sure. Won't be able to keep you home without tyin' you down. Mr. Big Shot."

"It would help if I had a car." Mamu didn't even look at me. She just sat there rocking as though she didn't hear a word we said, concentrating on the moon. I turned to Osceola.

"You're wastin' your breath, Mr. Big Shot." He laughed.

"It just don't seem possible that you're seventeen years old. Four years and you'll be able to vote." Priddie shook her head. "Where in the world does the time go? The days seem to last forever, but the years just fly by. Ain't that right, Miz Adela?"

"He can drive Irina to the buck," said Mamu and took a sip of her coffee. "There's plenty of work for you to do around here, Mr. Flowers." She seemed content that night, in spite of what had happened at the breakfast table. There didn't seem to be anything festering in her mind. I decided she had probably had at least two quick glasses of sherry.

After we took the dishes into the kitchen, Estella and I, against Mamu's protests, took another tray to the shack. It was almost dark and I led the way along the path with a kerosene lantern. Uncle Josh was sitting at the end of the dock in the half-light and the food, which I had left earlier, was crawling with bugs. He hadn't touched any of it.

On the way there I told Estella that the murdered woman had been a friend of his.

"When?" she asked.

"In college. He knew her when he was at Princeton."

"Has he seen her since? He must have to get this upset." She answered her own question. "I mean if it was just somebody he knew twenty years ago it wouldn't have thrown him for a loop like this, would it?"

"He didn't say if he's seen her since. All he said was that he knew her. Ssh, he'll hear us talking."

"You shouldn't have brought any food. I'm not hungry," he said as he saw us coming with the tray. The light from the lantern lit up the trees overhead and we were in a great, yellowish green cave that shimmered with the movement of the leaves.

"But you didn't eat anything at all today. At least have a few bites of the sandwich." Estella held the plate out to him.

"No, I couldn't."

"I brought you a piece of my birthday cake. It's chocolate. Your favorite. Priddie made it fresh this afternoon."

"Oh, that's right! It's your birthday today. Well, have a happy birthday, Ben, and many, many more. I've got something for you." He got up and went into the shack, emerging a moment later with a small dark book which he handed to me. "It's a guide to Venice. There's a map in there. Very detailed. It's not a first edition. In fact, it's a seventh and it was printed in 1907. Thirty-two years ago. But I don't expect Venice has changed much since then. Look," he said opening the book and holding it close to the lantern, "*John T. Phelan, Hotel Daniele, Venice. 4 May, 1910.* I like his handwriting. I wonder who he is . . . or was. I don't know how or where I got this book. And the price is right there. Three shillings and sixpence. So we know Mr. Phelan probably bought this in England. I wonder if he was American or an Englishman. I see someone's name in an old book and I imagine all sorts of things about him. Do you do that?" There was a hint of his usual glow. It was the talk of books that did it. He didn't wait for an answer to his question. "You'll go to Venice, someday. You will, I know it. The Canal Grande, the Piazza San Marco, Murano. . . . " The glow faded and he stopped talking.

"Thanks, Uncle Josh." It didn't seem like enough. "Thank you, very much. I'll read it. I really will." The conversation ended. "Are we going to swim?" I asked. As soon as I said it I knew it was a stupid question, but I was trying to return to some familiar ground, some kind of normalcy.

"You can if you want." He answered as though it was a perfectly reasonable thing for me to ask.

"It's nice to swim in the lamp light," I said trying to get him enthusiastic about something.

"I think I'm going to go in and lie down." He got up and walked along the dock. "I have a headache. But go ahead and swim. It won't bother me. I'm just not in the mood." He went into the shack and closed the door and Estella and I stood there for a moment before deciding it was best to leave him alone.

"I don't feel much like swimming, anyway," she said.

"Neither do I."

"Come on, let's take this stuff back to the house."

"Thanks again for the book," I called.

He didn't answer.

Later that night I waited on the porch for mother to come home so I could thank her for the ring. It was almost ten o'clock when she came walking slowly down Broadway in the bright moonlight. She was smiling as she came up on the porch and I realized I had forgotten what a handsome woman she was because I was usually so annoyed at her for acting so stupidly.

"Mother, I like the ring. . . . "

"Oh, I'm so glad, Ben. Let me see. Oh, yes, it looks like it belongs on your hand. It fits?"

"Yes, it fits just fine. It's beautiful."

"They call it a cat's eye, but it's really chrysoberyl. At least that's what the jeweler said. I memorized it. I'm probably not saying it right."

"I really like it."

"Well, I'm so glad." She almost hugged me, but thought better of it and just touched the ring on my hand. "I'm going up to bed. I'm exhausted." She started singing. "Happy birthday to you, happy birthday to you, happy birthday, dear Ben. . . . " She laughed and didn't finish the song.

I was going to tell her everything that happened that day with Uncle Josh but, as she started into the house, I was torn by the old nagging question of loyalty. If I told her about his reaction to the murders would I have to tell her he knew Gloria Gardiner? And would I be betraying Uncle Josh if I did? I decided he'd tell her himself if he wanted her to know. She'd find out soon enough anyway, so I just wished her a good night.

It was early the next morning when Estella's question about the last time Uncle Josh had seen Gloria Gardiner was, in a way, answered. Priddie and I, with the help of the geese and a little yellow bantam hen, so dedicated to motherhood she almost always had a brood of sassy chicks, were weeding the flower garden when the police car drove up with Adam and Sheriff Anderson. Mother had gone to work before any of us got up and Osceola was somewhere in the fields plowing.

"Morning, Ben. Morning, Priddie. I think it's going to be a little cooler today." Adam unfolded himself as he got out of the car. Sheriff Anderson sat looking at some papers for a moment and by the time he got out Mamu had appeared on the porch.

"What are you doing here so early?" she asked.

"Mrs. Wayland," the sheriff tipped his hat, "we'd like to talk to your brother." He was an imposing man somewhere in his fifties who wore very thick glasses and a meticulously trimmed and waxed mustache. His skin was prematurely wrinkled and mottled from too much sun.

"About what?" She folded her arms across her bosom and assumed her fighting stance.

"Well . . . ah . . ." he hesitated a moment, "we have some business with him. Where is he?"

"Ben, go get your uncle."

"No," said the sheriff. "Just tell us where he is?"

Estella, who had been working at the stand and saw the car drive by, came running down Broadway.

"What's going on, Adam?"

Before he could answer Mamu said, "He's down by the creek. That's where he lives. Ben will take you there."

"That won't be necessary. Just tell us how to get there, please." The "please" was emphatic and non-negotiable. Mamu glared. She didn't like not being in complete control. It was a circumstance she wasn't used to.

"Just follow the path to the left of the barn," I said. "It leads right to his shack."

"Thank you." They started off and Adam turned to us, raising his hands apologetically.

When they were out of sight Mamu turned to me. "You know what this is about?"

"No." I didn't want to tell her that Uncle Josh had been a friend of Gloria Gardiner. It would have infuriated her that we hadn't already told her what we knew.

"Estella, do you know why they're here? Officer Stoner is your friend. You talk to him on the phone. Did he say anything to you?"

"I don't talk to him on the phone, Mamu. I called him once. That's all. And I don't know why they're here."

"Well, it doesn't surprise me." She went into the house, slamming the door behind her.

"I'm going to ring for Osceola," said Priddie. She started for the brass ship's bell hanging on the porch that was rung whenever there was reason to call someone in from the fields

Mamu appeared behind the screen. "No one is going to ring for anyone. There's work to be done. Estella, go back to the stand right this minute. Now!"

It was almost an hour before the sheriff and Adam came back with Uncle Josh walking between them. Priddie had left me to finish the weeding and had gone into the house to discuss the situation with Mamu. Uncle Josh looked pale and sickly with huge dark circles around his eyes. He hadn't shaved and he was slumped over like a man who has beaten himself down. He was carrying the heavy burden of a dark secret. I knew that much. Obviously, Priddie and Mamu had been watching for them because as soon as Adam and the sheriff came around the house with Uncle Josh, they appeared on the porch.

"Where are you taking him?" It was a command from Mamu more than a question.

"Just down to the station."

"You tell me right this minute what this is all about. I demand to know." Mamu was furious with everyone. "Josh, what is going on?"

"It's all right, Adela, they. . . ."

"He's going to come with us," interrupted the sheriff. "We just want to ask him a few questions."

"I'll be back before you know it," said Uncle Josh. I ran down the walk and grabbed his arm and all he said, very quietly, was, "It should have been me, Ben." His eyes were the eyes of a dead man. He got in the back seat of the car, Adam and the sheriff got in the front, and they drove off without any further explanation. Uncle Josh didn't look at us, but Adam smiled sadly as they went down Broadway.

We sat by the phone all morning waiting to hear something, but every time it rang it was business. Orders for tomatoes and corn and cantaloupe. It was our busiest time of the year. By noon, when we still hadn't heard anything, I called the police station and it was Margaret Breedlove who answered.

"Your uncle's not here, Ben. Adam and the sheriff took him to Laurelwood. It's the county seat you know."

"When will he be back?"

"They didn't say. Imagine your uncle being involved in all this! You know, I never saw him before. Never. The people in town just talk about him as this hermit who lives on the creek. I couldn't believe it when I saw how good-looking he is. If he cut his hair he'd look like Tyrone Power. I mean it, he would. And him, carrying on with that woman. . . ."

"What are you talking about?"

"What are they saying? Who are you talking to?" Mamu tried to grab the phone out of my hand, but I held on to it.

"Oops, I shouldn't have said that." Margaret giggled. "Police business, don't you know. Well, anyway, it looks like he was carrying on with that woman. You know, the dead woman. That Mrs. Gardiner. Least that's what I heard the sheriff say to Adam. You never know, do you? I thought she was carrying on with that musical fella. You know, the singer. And her a married woman and all. Of course, being as good looking as your uncle is he could probably have any woman he wanted. And she was just beautiful. Did you see her picture in the paper? Like a movie star. How come so many rich people are good looking? You'd think having all that money would be enough."

I wanted to tell her to shut up. "I don't blame her messing around with your uncle, though. He could put his shoes under my bed any time he wanted. I'm just awful, aren't I?" She laughed again.

"Why are they saying all this?"

"What are they saying? Give me that phone." Again Mamu tried to take the phone, but I held on to it.

"Oh, well," Margaret assumed her confidential tone of voice, "they have witnesses that saw his rowboat slipping into the Gardiner boathouse late at night. A lot of the summer people said so. The sheriff questioned everybody that has a place on the lake. I guess the rowboat wasn't the only thing slipping in, if you get my drift. Anyway, . . ."

I hung up the phone

"What was all that about?" demanded Mamu.

"He's not there. They took him to Laurelwood." I was so overwhelmed by what Margaret had said I could barely speak.

"Who were you talking to?"

"Margaret Breedlove."

"What else did she say?"

"Nothing important. Well, you know her. She never shuts up." I wasn't about to say anything more than I had to.

"Tell Osceola to get the truck," she said without a moment's hesitation. "We're going to Laurelwood right now. This is ridiculous." She patted her hair to make sure there were no strands out of place. "I have to get my pocketbook."

"I'll go with you." Estella was anxious to find out what happened to Uncle Josh.

"No, you won't. You and Priddie stay here and look after things. And you get down to the stand. Those Hungarians can't count to two, let alone speak English. Tell them to turn the compost heap. I've been after them all week to do it. Priddie, if the phone rings answer it but if it's business . . . you know, orders, tell them to call back. Lord, I wish you'd learn to read and write." She went off to get her purse and I went to find Osceola.

Chapter VII

"I can't believe it. It just ain't possible Mr. Josh bein' mixed up in a murder." Osceola repeated it over and over as we drove to Laurelwood.

"I wish you'd stop saying that. No one's saying he's mixed up in a murder," said Mamu. "And keep your eyes on the road. You are the worst driver I've ever seen. You drive like a madman. Honestly!"

"I drive just fine. Anyway, I ain't sayin' he did the murder. I just mean the police think he knows somethin' he can tell them. Otherwise you tell me why they takin' him in for questions? You understand? That's what being mixed up means."

I still hadn't told them what Margaret Breedlove said. It seemed completely out of the question. Uncle Josh carrying on with one of the summer people. I just couldn't believe it. Yet, it did explain the way he acted when he heard she had been murdered. But it was the mention of Marius Dorfman that first upset him. That's when he spilled the sugar. It was all too much to digest and I didn't want to be the one to tell Mamu so I thought I'd just keep quiet and let Sheriff Anderson explain what was going on. It was the way we dealt with things in the family. We all had years of experience not saying anything.

Laurelwood, with a population of about nine thousand people, was the closest "city" to Millersburg. A town obviously proud of its colonial roots, it was an important stagecoach stop in the late seventeenth century and later, became a trade center with a bustling market square well into the early nineteen hundreds. Now the square had become a park with only an historical marker to commemorate its past and in the center, the white granite county courthouse with the police station in the basement.

Osceola parked the truck in one of the spaces reserved for police business and the three of us went into the station. It was close to noon when we got there and the sergeant behind the desk, a balding man with a bulbous nose, was eating his lunch.

"Yes?" he said with a mouthful of food. "What can I do for you?"

"I want to talk to someone about my brother," said Mamu. "I understand he's been brought here."

"Are you family?"

"I just said he was my brother. Pay attention."

The sergeant stiffened. "Well you're not all family." He pointed to Osceola. "He's not family, is he?"

"You don't got to be blood to be family."

"Well, you do here." He put down his sandwich and turned to Mamu. "What's your brother's name?"

"Pritchard. Joshua Pritchard."

"Oh, yeah. Sit down over there and I'll see what I can find out. I don't know if he can have visitors."

"I would like to see the chief of police . . . or whoever is in charge. Right this minute."

"I said to sit down. Pay attention."

I thought Mamu was going to hit him. Osceola took her by the arm and steered her away from the desk.

"Just relax, Miz Adela. The man said he is goin' to try to find out what's goin' on." He almost whispered. "Rule number one is you don't get the police mad at you. You hear me? Listen to what I'm sayin' for a change." He half pushed Mamu onto the bench where she sat fuming. "You ain't the boss here, you know."

We couldn't hear what the sergeant was mumbling into the phone but, before he finally put the receiver down he said, "What was your name again?"

"Wayland. Adela Pritchard Wayland. My brother is Joshua Pritchard. Can you remember that?"

"Wayland," he said and hung up. "Somebody will be down in a few minutes." He went back to eating his sandwich.

"I'll see to it that he loses his job." Mamu took Osceola's advice and almost whispered.

It was about ten minutes before a young policeman came from somewhere in the back of the station.

"Sorry to keep you waiting. I'm Officer Harling. Are you Mrs. Wayland?"

We all got up and went to him.

"What is going on, that's what I'd like to know. Where's Officer Stoner and Sheriff Anderson?"

"I think they've gone back to Millersburg."

"And they left Joshua here?"

"Just come with me and we'll try to straighten everything out." He turned to Osceola, "I'm afraid you'll have to wait here. Sorry."

"That's ridiculous," said Mamu.

"Family only. Those are the rules, Mrs. Wayland."

The sergeant behind the desk smiled broadly.

"You go on, Miz Adela. I'll wait out by the truck."

Officer Harling asked, "Are you eighteen? You have to be eighteen."

"Yes," I lied, "my birthday was yesterday."

"Eighteen already. It's hard to believe." Mamu smiled.

"Please come this way."

Officer Harling showed us to a dingy little room with a scarred wooden table and four battered chairs. Incongruously, in the center of the table was a wilted white rose in half a glass of water. The place reeked of stale tobacco and coffee. We waited for almost an hour before an older man, wearing a brown rumpled suit, came in. While we were waiting Mamu said very little. She was obviously uneasy by what was happening and I could see it in her face. This was something with which she had never had to deal and with all her bluster she was on very shaky ground. I had never seen her in a situation where she didn't know what she was doing.

"I'm sorry to keep you waiting," he said. "Things are very hectic around here today. I'm Detective Wilson. Would you like some coffee?"

"I'd like to know why my brother is being detained here."

"Well, to get right to the point, we're holding him for questioning about the Miller Lake murders."

"Joshua! What would he know about the murders? That's absolutely preposterous."

"He was seen going into the Gardiner's boathouse at night."

"The night of the murders?" asked Mamu.

"Well, we're not exactly certain of that. But there's a very good possibility."

I started to feel sick because suddenly everything Margaret Breedlove had said was probably right.

"What in the world would Joshua be doing going into their boathouse? He doesn't even know those people."

"We think he does. Especially the late Mrs. Gardiner. We think he knew her very well. But he won't tell us anything."

"Knew her very well? Are you implying. . . ."

"That your brother had a relationship with Mrs. Gardiner. Yes, Mrs. Wayland. There's a very good possibility."

"All these possibilities," said Mamu suspiciously. "Has my brother talked about this? About knowing these people?"

"No. As I already told you, he won't say anything. That's why we're keeping him here. He's hiding something, I know that much. Otherwise, he'd tell us what he knows. We know he went to the Gardiner house often. We have witnesses."

Mamu stared at the floor for a moment and very calmly said, "I want to see him."

"OK."

As he started out of the room, Mamu said, "How long are you going to keep him here?"

"I don't know. Unless he says something we feel we have reason to. If he was having a relationship with the deceased . . . well, there was another man murdered. Not her husband. Do you see what I'm getting at? Jealousy is a powerful motive."

"Yes. Thank you." I could actually see the color drain from her face.

"If he was my brother I'd tell him to cooperate with the police. In the long run it might go easier on him."

"Aren't you jumping to conclusions, Detective Wilson?"

"Perhaps I am, Mrs. Wayland. Perhaps I am." And he left.

I don't know what Mamu was thinking but she remained silent for several minutes and I knew I shouldn't say anything. Finally she looked at me. "Maybe I should talk to him alone? Maybe he'd prefer that? We'll ask him. Do you understand, Ben?"

"Sure. I understand. I really do."

A few minutes later Detective Wilson brought him into the room. He looked worse than he had earlier in the day.

"Take your time," the detective said just before he left us alone. "Talk things out."

Uncle Josh sat across the table from us, keeping his eyes averted.

"Would you prefer talking to me alone?"

"No. Ben can hear what I have to say." He took a deep breath. "I'm sorry about all this, Adela."

"Yes . . . well . . . I'd like an explanation."

"I didn't kill Gloria."

"Gloria? Then you did know her."

"Oh, yes."

"Did you have a relationship with her?"

"I was in love with her. I've always been in love with her. Seems like my whole life."

Mamu shook her head in disbelief. "I am, to say the least, astounded by this, Josh. Have you any idea how extraordinary this information is to me?"

"Adela. . . ."

"Tell me everything because I don't know what to do. I'm completely at a loss. I simply do not know what to do. And I mean everything, Josh."

"Yes." It was almost as if he couldn't catch his breath and I felt if he went on he'd start gasping for air. He took several deep breaths. "Well, I first met her when I was in college." He looked at me for a moment and must have realized that I had told Mamu nothing. "I met her at a house party weekend at the Ivy Club. She was luminous. boyish . . . stylishly boyish. Short blond hair, practically no bust, long tan legs . . . she could have stepped off the cover of a fashion magazine." He turned to me. "No matter what anyone ever tells you, Ben, there is such a thing as love at first sight."

"That's beside the point." Mamu was uncomfortable when the word love came into any conversation.

"No, it isn't, Adela. It's not beside the point at all. You said you wanted to know everything. Well, how and when we fell in love is part of what I have to say. You have to understand what we meant to one another and what it was like, the only time in my life to be half of a perfect whole. That's what Whitman called it. Being half of a perfect whole. I had that, Adela. I had that!" He was annoyed with Mamu and I could hear it in his voice as he directed whatever he had to say to me for the next few minutes. "You have no idea what it's like to be half of a perfect whole. And then, when the other half is gone. . . ." He couldn't talk for a moment and his eyes brimmed with tears. "I only exchanged a few words with her that first time we met. I don't think anyone formally introduced us, but we started talking and we both knew something extraordinary was happening. We only talked a few moments because I couldn't think of anything to say. Neither could she. We ran into each other several more times over the next few months. She was always with a group of girls from Vassar. I didn't like most of her friends. They were snobs . . . you know the sort . . . the kind of people who wait in ambush to hear French words mispronounced so they can pounce on the poor ignoramus. So shallow they confuse pronunciation with intellect. But Gloria wasn't like that. Did I say she was a music major? She wanted to compose." He looked at me and his eyes brightened. "It was Gloria who introduced me to Mozart and Beethoven and Franz Liszt. You know, Ben, the Second Hungarian Rhapsody. We have her to thank for SchumannandhisClara. I heard some of Gloria's work and she was very good. You would have liked her, Ben." He turned to Mamu. "She was beautiful, Adela. *Is* . . ." He looked away a moment and took another deep breath. "*Was* beautiful. Jesus Christ!" He put his head down for a moment and I could see his whole body shudder. I looked at Mamu and she sat there registering nothing, just staring at him. I wanted her to reach out and comfort him but I knew she wouldn't.

"Go on," she said after a moment.

"We started seeing one another . . . meeting weekends in New York at the Astor. Those years after the war were exciting, weren't they, Adela? The beginning of the Roaring Twenties. They certainly did roar. Everything had changed. New York was wonderful. Wonderful and dangerous. Bursting with energy. We'd go to musical shows and then have a late supper and afterward we'd walk through Central Park and dance and sing, doing all the numbers we had just seen. We really had such good times." He looked at us for a moment before going on. "Gloria was from Pittsburgh. Her family was in steel. Fulton Steel. Because of her father she had connections with a lot of important people in New York. The Fultons were patrons of the arts and Gloria grew up knowing so many famous artists. She led a very privileged life. We once went to a party for F. Scott Fitzgerald. It was when *This Side of Paradise* was published. I was introduced to him." He turned to me. "I never told you I met Fitzgerald, did I, Ben?"

"No, you never mentioned that." There was the hint of the old glow in his eyes and it broke my heart.

"You never mentioned that to anyone," said Mamu, pointedly. Not that she would have cared one way or the other about his meeting F. Scott Fitzgersald or the pope, for that matter.

"Well, I did. I met him. And Zelda, of course. And Dorothy Parker. Odd little woman, I thought. She blew cigarette smoke in my face. I don't know whether she did it on purpose or not. So many . . . very famous people . . . were there. It was a wonderful party." He got up and moved to the window where he stood looking out. "Gloria and I were so in love . . . there is nothing like it . . . that feeling of wanting to be a part of every cell, every atom of the other person. Of never having enough of them . . . never being sated. But it ended when her father found out. I was from a family of no consequence and my future wasn't particularly promising." He looked at Mamu. "Oh, I was connected with money because you were married to Byard Wayland. But I was not, as Dickens said, 'a young man with great expectations.'" He took Gloria out of school and sent her to Europe with an aunt as a chaperone, for the grand tour. People did that in those days when they wanted to get their children out of the country and away from someone they considered undesirable. Maybe they still do? We wrote for awhile, but I think all my letters were intercepted because she never referred to anything I said and kept asking me to write. Finally, her letters stopped coming. A few years later, she met Claude Gardiner. He was from a good family, very old money, and exactly what her father wanted in a son-in-law. It didn't matter that she wasn't in love with him. So, they were married."

"You said you lost touch with her."

"I did, until early spring . . . not this past spring but the year before. I ran into her on Little Sister."

Miller Lake had two islands. Grand, which was about an acre, and Little Sister, which was half that size. How and when they were named no one knew, but both islands were popular in summer, when people picnicked there, and in winter when skaters built bonfires to warm themselves.

"I had been watching a pair of mallards going and coming from the island so I rowed in to see if I could find a nest. The drake carried on as I got closer so I did see where they were nesting even though the hen was camouflaged so perfectly I never would have seen her if he hadn't given her away. I didn't want to disturb her so I sat enjoying the early spring warmth of the sun for a while as the drake scolded me for trespassing. Then I heard her laugh. After all those years I knew right away it was Gloria. It occurred to me that I might be imagining I heard her because, over the years, she had come to mind at the oddest times and for no apparent reason." He took a deep breath. "At the sound of her voice, all the memories came back in a rush. I walked along the shore and there she was with a young boy . . . her son. They had their shoes off and were trying to muster the courage to wade out into the ice-cold water. She was as beautiful as ever."

"And you've been seeing her ever since?"

"Whenever she was at the lake. Yes. They live in New York. Her husband doesn't like the lake so he's rarely here." He came back to the table and sat.

"She was a married woman," said Mamu. "How could you be so foolish?"

"Foolish! Adela, you astound me! I was in love with her, for God's sake. There was nothing foolish about it. And she was in a miserable marriage. She was very unhappy. There was no love in that marriage. None at all. Well, you know what that's like, Adela. How terrible it is to be in a loveless marriage." Mamu stiffened. Her apparent lack of understanding angered him. "You were in one for thirty years." It was the first time I ever heard Uncle Josh say anything about Mamu's relationship with my grandfather other than the often-told amusing story of their courtship in Atlantic City.

She glanced at me, sorry that I was there to hear, I was sure. "This isn't about me, Josh, it's about you. What about the tenor?"

"She hardly knew him. She had talked to him a few times on the phone and that was the only contact they had until that night. They were going to co-chair a fundraising gala for the opera. It was their first meeting. They were getting together to make plans, that's all. She told me he was driving down from New York. The poor bastard. Oh, God! Shit! When I think about it. . . ." He buried his head in his hands. He said something which we couldn't understand.

"What did you say?" asked Mamu.

He looked up. "No one saw me go into the boathouse that night because I didn't go. I wasn't there. I knew she was meeting with Marius Dorfman and I stayed away. Detective Wilson said there are witnesses. That's impossible because I was not there." Having made his point emphatically, he leaned back in the chair. "It was Claude who killed them. Jesus, when I think about it. So horrible! The sheer terror of those last few minutes of life. It should have been me. I wish it had been."

"Stop that," Mamu snapped. "We've got enough to deal with. We don't need that kind of talk. Now, did he know about you and his wife?"

"Gloria said he was suspicious of her seeing someone. He accused her but she denied it, for the boy's sake. If it wasn't for the boy she would have left Claude. They had terrible fights. He was a vicious man. He didn't want her, but he didn't want anyone else to have her."

"How do you know her husband was the murderer? How can you be sure it was him?"

"By the way they were murdered. Claude Gardiner spent a great deal of time in Africa. The family was in diamonds. He traveled all over the world, but Gloria told me he was particularly fond of Africa because he spent so much time there. Well, I've read a lot about Africa and I read that certain tribes, when they killed their enemies, put the genitals in the mouths of the dead men. It was ritualistic. It's what he would have done. It's what he did. I know he killed them."

"Why haven't you told all this to Detective Wilson?"

That's what I wanted to know. "Tell him. Tell him now and maybe he'll let you come home with us."

Mamu looked at me as though I had said something embarrassingly idiotic and I realized, of course, that I had.

"I don't want to drag Gloria's name through the mud."

Mamu was losing her patience. "It's a little late for that, isn't it? The radio and newspapers are suggesting all kinds of things about the two of them. The Gardiner woman and the tenor, I mean."

"That will be cleared up. Too many people . . . his manager, the people at the opera . . . his wife, if he has one . . . know why he was there that night. But if I say anything about our relationship. . . . Well, I just can't do it. When I think of that boy . . . finding the bodies . . . he doesn't have to see his mother dragged through the mud. I can't do it, Adela. I won't."

"You've been a fool, Josh, but there's no reason to keep on being a fool."

Uncle Josh smiled. "Do you have any idea what it's like to really love someone, Adela?" She didn't answer. "You don't know what you've missed."

"Come on, Ben," she said and walked out of the room. Uncle Josh reached across the table and I took his hand for a moment before following Mamu.

Detective Wilson was in the hall talking to another policeman. "Well?" he asked, stomping his cigarette out on the floor.

"Well, what?" Mamu replied, and kept right on walking.

On our way out of the courthouse she suggested I drive because Osceola would be upset when she told him what was happening and he tended to drive too fast when something bothered him. I was happy to drive, as always, and happy to have something to concentrate on. Mamu told Osceola everything that Uncle Josh had said except, of course, the part about her not knowing what love was. I didn't pay much attention because my mind was reeling, full of diamond mines and dancing in Central Park and F. Scott Fitzgerald and weekends at the Astor and, most of all, murder. The images were surreal and kaleidoscopic. In a way, I felt I had just listened to one of Uncle Josh's stories and I didn't know which character to focus on. He, of course, was the hero. He was always the hero, just as Estella was always the heroine. It didn't matter if it was fact or fiction. He was Heathcliff and Ahab, Launcelot and Dorian Gray, Jekyll and Hyde, Charles Lindbergh and Jesus Christ and she was Catherine Earnshaw and Emma Bovary, Amelia Earhart and Anna Karenina, Juliet and the Virgin Mary. I knew them both in their naked perfection, he like an isolated, dark, lithe El Greco saint and she, Rodinesque, supple, complex, and flawless. There were no characters in books, no national icons that could compare with either one of them. But I wanted to know more about Gloria Fulton Gardiner, the tragic heroine of this particular story, and her murderous husband. And, as if that wasn't enough to occupy my thoughts, there was Mamu's thirty-year love-less marriage. I decided, just as we were approaching the Millersburg Mercantile, that she more than likely did kill my grandfather. As perverse as it may have been, I almost understood why she would do it. Apparently, love, or the lack of it, could motivate someone to kill! But I was seventeen and had no idea what love was all about, no idea how complicated and diverse it could be. Would there ever be a circumstance where Priddie would kill Osceola? It was possible although I couldn't imagine it. Or Estella kill Adam? I had to push the jumble out of my mind and at the same time I wanted to think about it. I wanted to have what Uncle Josh had with Gloria Gardiner. I was jealous of that. I was jealous of him. There he was, being held by the police and I was jealous.

But there was something else upsetting about the sudden aware-ness of Gloria Gardiner. Even though she was dead, she was a new thread in the fabric of our existence. For the rest of my life, whenever I thought of Uncle Josh I would have to think of her and I had no idea who she was. Until that time it had only been Mamu, mother, Osceola and Priddie, Estella, Uncle Josh, and me. A very small cast of characters in the drama and comedy of my life. He never told us about her, but I was sure he told her about us. I wanted to know what he told her. I had a feeling of a peculiar and unfair imbalance because the late Gloria Gardiner had the advantage. She was an intruder. I wanted to know her, but I never would.

I thought of what it must have been like, years after he had accepted the fact that he would never see her again, to sit in the sun on tiny Little Sister and suddenly hear her laugh. They could have gone on for the rest of their lives not knowing they were only a few miles apart. If it hadn't been for the mallards choosing that spot for the nest they never would have known. Could everything in life be predicated on something as tenuous as accident or coincidence? There probably would never ever be a moment in his life to match it. But, I also thought, knowing how vividly *I* could conjure up horrific images, what it must be like for him to picture her mutilated and bloody body. Those were the extremes he would have to live with. To make matters worse, he was suspected of killing the person he had loved all those years.

I heard the word "lawyer" mentioned several times, but I was too involved with my own thoughts to pay any attention. Mamu and Osceola, depending on one another to make decisions, as they did about Broadway Acres, were dealing with what had to be done while I was still lost in what had already taken place.

When we turned into our lane we saw the boys working the stand, which upset Mamu. They were sitting in the shade of the canopy having a cigarette.

"Good Lord," she said, "they'll be giving everything away! Get to work," she yelled. "They don't even know what the word means!" She looked at Osceola. "You should have fired them the day they started working."

The geese and guinea hens made the usual racket when they saw the truck coming down Broadway, and Sinclair, who never rested when anyone was away from home, whinnied from his corral. Priddie and Estella were waiting on the porch. Everything was as it should be and it annoyed the hell out of me that nothing had changed. I expected the world, especially our world, to be in ruins. But the sun was shining, the house was still gleaming white, the little yellow hen was scolding her chicks, and the flowers were in bloom. It didn't seem fair.

"Come inside," said Mamu to Priddie and Estella, "and I'll tell you everything. Ben, go down to the stand and send those idiots back to the field." She and Osceola went into the house with Priddie, and Estella and I started down Broadway. The pair of mourning doves was there and, as usual, when I came too close, shot into the air and whistled away over the trees. It was the first time I thought of what it must have been like for Uncle Josh locked away in a jail cell.

Chapter VIII

On the 3rd of September, Hitler declared war on Poland, but the banner headline in the *Millersburg Daily Reminder* read, "Suspect In Custody For Miller Lake Murders." The beginning of World War II was relegated to second place because whatever was happening way off in Europe really had little to do with what was going on in New Jersey. The story about the murder suspect didn't give much information, merely that the police, acting quickly and efficiently on information received, were holding someone and, also, because of the celebrity of Marius Dorfman, the FBI was on the case. It did say that Mr. Dorfman and Mrs. Gardiner were merely acquaintances who were working together for a charitable cause. That much was made perfectly clear. And that Mr. Claude Gardiner, husband of the deceased, who was in Tarrytown, New York, the night of the murders, visiting his nanny on her eighty-fourth birthday, was bereft.

"Well, I expect he is," said Mamu when she finished reading the article. "Visiting his nanny, my foot!" She really believed Uncle Josh was innocent and I was relieved to know that.

"Well, at least they didn't print Uncle Josh's name." Estella took the paper from Mamu and started to reread the article.

"That will happen soon enough," I said, "if Margaret Breedlove has anything to do with it. How come he's gone from being held for questioning to a suspect?"

"They have to have somebody, don't they?" Mamu shook her head in disgust.

"Ben, eat some breakfast," said Priddie.

"I don't want anything."

"I just feel so bad for Mr. Josh. Lord, how he must be hurtin'. How could anyone suspect a man like him, I just don't know." Priddie was grief-stricken. "The woman he loved, all cut up like that. How much can a body bear? Sometimes I have to question the ways of the Lord. I truly do. And I know I shouldn't. God forgive me."

"Well, I certainly question. I can tell you that much. How anyone in their right mind can believe. . . ."

"Don't start that not believin' in God stuff, Miz Adela, now just ain't the time." It was a warning and Mamu took heed.

Osceola stuck his head in the back door. "Today's the day Irina has to go to the buck. You goin' to take her, Ben?"

"Why are you standing in the doorway? Come in," said Mamu.

"I got mud on my shoes."

"Then you stay right where you are." Priddie took a step toward him. "I'm not in the mood to clean up after you or nobody else, today."

"Ben, you comin'? I'll help you load her in the truck."

"Go on, Ben," said Mamu. "No matter what's happened, there's work to be done. Life goes on, you know."

I didn't make a move because I didn't feel like doing anything. And I couldn't accept that life just goes on no matter what.

"I'll take her," said Estella, getting up from the table.

"No you won't." Mamu waved her down. "I've got plans for you today. We have to go over the accounts and you add better than anyone else does. So you just relax, Miss."

"Come on, boy. I got work to do. I can't wait around all day for you to make up your mind." Osceola sounded annoyed. I'm sure he was trying to get my mind off Uncle Josh. "Do I have to do everythin' around here?"

"All right."

"You ain't had a mouthful of breakfast," said Priddie as I went, pulling the screen door closed against the flies.

"I'll phone Mr. Colson and tell him you're on your way," called Mamu. "You drive carefully. I don't want anything to happen to my goat. Do you hear me?"

Goats, like most animals, are creatures of habit and don't like change and our goats, every one we ever had, hated getting into the truck. They screamed as if they were being taken to slaughter and the other goats screamed in sympathy and that started Sinclair and he started the geese and the chickens and it sounded like bloody murder. Osceola picked Irina up and put her in the bed of the truck, tying her securely.

"You got money for the stud fee?"

"No."

"You don't think that ol' Billy goat does it for free, do you? He ain't like the rest of us. He gets paid for doin' it." He laughed and gave me a handful of bills. It didn't seem very funny to me as I climbed behind the wheel. "And get some gas when you're out." He put his hand on my arm. "Listen to what I'm sayin', boy. Everythin' is goin' to be OK. Ain't nothin' goin' to happen to Mr. Josh. You got to believe that. We goin' to do what has to be done . . . get a lawyer . . . the best . . . you'll see. It's all goin' to work out just fine." I wasn't sure he really believed it. "You ain't a little kid no more. You're a man, so get on with things. Miz Adela is right when she says life goes on. It does, Ben, the world keeps twirlin' and nothin' can stop it. Not a goddamn thing can stop it. You just got to stand tall and keep on movin'."

I didn't want to hear anymore about the perpetuity of life and the resiliency of the spirit so I backed the truck out into the yard and started down Broadway.

"You be careful on the road," said Osceola, walking next to the truck. "It looks like it's clabberin' up to rain. You watch yourself. What do we got if we ain't got the truck."

I pushed my foot on the accelerator so he'd have to run if he wanted to keep up.

"You're gettin' mean now. I don't like that one little bit. Not one little bit. Try actin' like a grownup and remember what I said. Life goes on."

"Life may go on," I said as I pulled away, leaving him standing in the middle of the lane, " but I don't give a fuck."

"You watch your mouth Mr. Big Shot! Mean. Just plain mean. That's what you are." His voice faded away as I headed for the highway.

The Colson's farm was halfway between Millersburg and Laurelwood so I decided to drop Irina off and go on into Laurelwood, pick mother up on her lunch hour, and take her to see Uncle Josh. As I drove down their long and deeply rutted lane I could see Mrs. Colson, an enormous, comfortable woman, hanging up wash in the side yard. It was sparklingly white in contrast to all the junk that was lying around. Mr. Colson, a wiry little man who always looked like a cricket to me, liked cars as much as Osceola and had bits and pieces of dozens of them strewn all over the place. The house hadn't been painted in twenty years and the garden was completely out of control, but they seemed not to notice any of it. Apparently, they were happy as any two people could be, smiling, cheerful, and asking after the family.

"So, Ben, you must think I'm crazy," said Mrs. Colson as she came to the truck, trying to push her bright red hair back in place, "hanging up wash when there's going to be a downpour. I love what the rainwater does to the laundry. Especially the sheets. It makes them so soft."

"Ben doesn't care about laundry, do you, Ben?" said Mr. Colson good-naturedly.

"If you catch rain water in a bucket," she went on without paying any attention to him, "wash your hair in it. Nothing's better for the hair than rainwater. *Regen wasser,* the Germans call it. My grandmother was always collecting *Regen wasser.*" She didn't wait for my reaction to the rainwater suggestion. "So, look at you! Driving on your own! I've never seen you without Osceola. So, how's your pretty sister? And your grandma?"

"Fine, thank you, Mrs. Colson." She had met Estella several times but never Mamu and all I could think of was if Mamu had seen their place she never would have let her goats be serviced there.

"So, Osceola and his wife? They good? What's her name?"

"Priddie. They're fine, too."

"That's right, Priddie. I just love that name."

Mr. Colson climbed into the back of the truck to untie Irina. "So, which one of the girls is this one?" Like Mrs. Colson, he started most of his sentences with "So."

"This is Irina," I said.

"Irene, huh? So, is it Irene one, two, or three?"

"Number two."

"So, I'm sure Billy's anxious. He hasn't had a girlfriend for quite awhile." He winked at me, letting me know that it was a man's world and we could exchange innuendoes even as far as goats were concerned. I helped him get Irina out of the truck and she carried on worse than ever.

"I'm going into Laurelwood. If it's all right I'll be back this afternoon to get her. I'm going to have lunch with my mother." I don't know why I thought I had to tell them my plans. I just kept talking because I was afraid Mrs. Colson was going to ask about Uncle Josh and I wasn't going to tell her he was being held in jail.

"Well, isn't that nice." Mrs. Colson petted the goat, trying to calm her. "Such a pretty girl, we'll take good care of you, won't we?" she cooed. "So, how is your mother?" She had never met mother, either.

"She's fine."

"So, you go on," said Mr. Colson, "before Emily talks your ear off. Once she gets started you can't shut her up." He smiled and patted her on her ample rump. "Have a good time with your mother and I'll look after Irene."

As I drove down the lane to the main road, I could hear Irina screaming even louder as she saw the truck disappearing, I'm sure, feeling totally abandoned, and I could smell the powerful, musky odor of the Billy goat even though he was nowhere to be seen.

I hadn't been to Schiller's Lumber since a few years after mother started working, but I knew it was on County Line Road on the west side of Laurelwood. There was no missing it as I got close because their sign was a carpenter about twenty feet tall with a gigantic hammer raised as if to strike a nail. I pulled into the lot, parked the truck, and as I walked to the office I could hear low rumblings of thunder off in the distance and the sky was getting heavier and darker by the minute. The air was so humid it was almost liquid. In the office, two ceiling fans were lazily spinning and not doing a bit of good to cool things off. Like the lumberyard, the office had the resiny and rich smell of wood. There were ashtrays full of cigarette butts on the counter along with dusty samples of different woods and a hand-printed notice of tools on sale. Along the right wall were kegs of nails, samples of bricks, and several dog-eared blueprints tacked to the wall. A few flies hovered in the center of the room chasing each other, but they were the only signs of life. I waited a few minutes and decided to tap the "ring for service" chrome bell on the counter.

"I didn't know anyone was here," said a tall, thin man with a shock of graying hair as he came out of a back room cleaning his glasses with his shirttail. "Has it started raining yet?"

"No, sir. But it looks like it's going to any minute."

"That's OK. We need it. It will cool things down before we all die from the heat. What can I do for you, son?" He slipped the glasses on and smiled.

"I'd like to speak to Mrs. Whyte."

"Eulalie Whyte? Oh, she doesn't work here anymore. No, no, she hasn't worked here for must be two, three years now."

He might just as well have slapped me across the face. I stared at him for a moment, unable to open my mouth until, finally, I recovered enough to ask, "Do you know where she is?"

"No idea. She called one day and said she wouldn't be in and I thought she meant for the day, but she said she wouldn't be in ever again. She thanked me, apologized, and that was it. She came by to pick up the money we owed and we never heard a word from her again."

"Well. . . ." was about all I could say. I was so dumbfounded I could feel my throat closing.

"I can give you her phone number in Millersburg. I'm sure I've got it here somewhere. It will take me awhile to find it. She lives in Millersburg, you know."

"Yeah, I know. Thanks. I don't need the number."

I almost staggered on my way out of the office and back to the truck. I climbed in and sat there for the longest time, absolutely senseless. I know I was incapable of touch, taste, smell, sight, and hearing. Everything in me shut down and I don't remember thinking about anything. When I *could* think the first thing that came to mind was, "Where the hell does she go every day?" Somehow, sometime later, I managed to start the truck and pull out, but I had no idea where I was going. I remember driving down County Line Road back the way I had come and nothing else until I parked the truck near the intersection of Laurel and Emmerson streets, which was the center of town. I sat looking at strangers passing by, probably thinking that if I waited long enough mother would walk by and I'd get some explanation. What could she possibly have been doing all these years?, I thought. And why *wouldn't* she tell us? It was totally incomprehensible.

I must have been there for an hour before I decided to visit Uncle Josh. As I drove to the courthouse I thought, as much as I wanted to tell him about mother . . . to tell anyone about her because I was bursting with this extraordinary discovery . . . I wouldn't. He had enough to worry about. But as it turned out, I wasn't even tempted because they wouldn't let me see him.

"Not today," said the young Officer Harling when he finally came out to the desk to talk to me. The same bulbous-nosed policeman, dripping with sweat, was sitting there reading a magazine. "The FBI is here and he can't see anyone. Tell your grandmother to call tomorrow."

By the time I got back to the truck I realized how hungry I was. I hadn't eaten anything all day. With everything that was happening I didn't think I was supposed to be hungry. Osceola and Mamu saying "life goes on" flashed through my mind. Instead of trying to find another parking place on the street, I left the truck there and walked across the park to the Rexall Drug Store to get a sandwich. Even the indestructible geraniums and dusty miller edging the walkways criss-crossing the courthouse were looking wilted. Every bench in the park in a shady spot was occupied. Mothers with toddlers, old men telling stories, and young men in shirtsleeves, obviously on their lunch hour, flirting with girls in filmy summery dresses. No one seemed to be worried about the threatening storm clouds.

I could have counted the number of times I had eaten in a restaurant on two hands and most of the restaurants were little fishermen's hangouts Osceola took us to when we went to the shore. They could hardly have been classified as restaurants. I was very uncomfortable eating in public and eating alone was a new and unpleasant experience. There were six tables, all crowded with people laughing and chatting while they had their meal. I was glad there were no empty seats because I wouldn't have been able to sit with strangers anyway. There was an unoccupied stool at the counter between a pretty young woman in a flowered dress who was fanning herself with the menu and an older woman in a nurse's uniform who kept pulling it away from her skin, trying to get a little air circulating.

"Yes?" asked the girl behind the counter. She drew a pencil from the ugly brown snood holding her blond hair in place and touched the point to her tongue, preparing to write. Her lipstick was the reddest I had ever seen. She was preoccupied with everyone else in the place and never once looked my way while she was taking my order. "Do you know what you want or do you need a menu?"

"I'll have a bacon, lettuce, and tomato sandwich."

"One BLT. White or wheat?"

"White or wheat?

"Bread."

"Oh. White."

"Toast?"

"Yeah, toast."

"Anything to drink?"

"Water, please." I wasn't sure I had enough money for the stud fee, gas, lunch, and a tip. Osceola told us to always leave a tip because waitresses and waiters depended on tips for their living seeing as how they worked for slave wages. Most everyone in the place was involved with their lunches, but I felt they were all looking at me, waiting for me to make some terrible faux pas, but by the time my sandwich arrived I was so engrossed in thoughts of mother I wasn't paying attention to anyone.

If she hadn't already told us what she was doing every day and where she was going she probably wouldn't tell me the truth if I confronted her. As much as I wanted to tell someone, until I really knew what it was all about, I didn't know what good the telling would do. I thought if I followed her when she supposedly went to work the next day I'd at least see if she was getting on the bus, and where she got off. But I didn't know how I was going to get the use of the truck again, unless I didn't pick Irina up at the Colsons' until the next morning. Mamu would have a fit if Irina was away from home for the night, I knew that much. And I couldn't think of a reason not to pick her up, but then there was a crash of thunder and I started to devise a plan. I paid for my sandwich, left a ten-cent tip, and went outside and stood under the awning watching people running to get out of the rain. It was torrential, with raindrops slamming on the sidewalk and jumping around like bits of broken crystal. The clouds, black and ominous, were moving slowly so I knew we were in for a good long storm.

"This is going to last all day," said a stocky man in a wilted seersucker suit and straw boater who had taken refuge.

"I hope so," I said as I walked out into the downpour, dodging cars on Laurel Street, then ambled my way across the park until I got back to the truck. I was wet through to the skin, but I needed to kill a little more time before I called home so I sat in the truck listening to the rain beating on the roof, thinking about mother. It was raining so hard the storm drains couldn't handle all the water and for a short time the parking lot was flooded. That was reason enough to make my first phone call.

"Can I use your phone?" I asked the policeman behind the desk. "I'm stuck in the parking lot. It's flooded."

"Boy, you are drenched. I thought you left a long time ago."

"I went to get some lunch. I want to call home."

He looked at me for a minute trying to decide whether or not to let me use it. "I'm not supposed to do this, but . . . OK. Just make it snappy."

Mamu answered the phone, something she never did if there was anyone else available. I had expected Estella or Priddie so I was shocked to hear her voice. I told her I had stopped by to see Uncle Josh and was stuck in the parking lot. She started to get upset because Irina was at the Colsons' all that time, but I changed the subject by telling her about the FBI and not being able to see Uncle Josh. She carried on for a bit and then I thought I'd better lay the groundwork for what I was going to tell her later.

"You know, the lane up to the Colson place is rutted so bad you can hardly get up there when it's dry. I don't know. . . ."

"Well, you can't leave that poor goat there. She'll die of fright. She won't know what's going on."

"I'll try but it's pretty muddy."

"Don't go doing anything foolish." It was much easier than I expected. I wouldn't even have to make a second call home. "Osceola will have a conniption fit if anything happens to that truck. You be careful."

"Nothing is going to happen to the truck. I'll call you later if I have to." I hung up and left the police station.

When the flooding subsided a bit I drove out of the lot and headed for a gas station on the way back to Millersburg. I drove past Colson's lane first and it was a raging river of mud. I didn't have to lie; I couldn't have gotten the truck up to the house. When I got to the gas station I called and asked Mrs. Colson if it would be all right if I picked up Irina the next day. She said it would be fine and not to worry. They'd take good care of her. Then I filled the gas tank and went home.

The rain slackened by late afternoon, but it was about eight-thirty that night when it completely stopped and a white moon slid out from behind the clouds. Mamu carped about the goat all through dinner, but by the time we had our coffee she accepted Irina's being away for the night as a cruel act of nature. Nature, cruel or not, had seen to it that I didn't have to lie to get the use of the truck the next day.

"Nothing can be done about it," conceded Mamu. "That's that."

"Life goes on," I mumbled. She didn't pick up on it, but Estella did and kicked me under the table. Kicking had always been our primary expression of camaraderie during dinner.

The other topic of conversation at the dinner table was Uncle Josh's lawyer. Or rather, the search for a lawyer for him. Mamu had called her cousin Alice and talked to her husband, who by then was Bishop Rigsby, about several prominent lawyers in his affluent congregation. He assured her that if they couldn't take the case, one or the other of them would know the right man. She made it perfectly clear that she wanted the best. She also made it clear that Uncle Josh was innocent of murder and only guilty of bad judgment and abject stupidity. Apparently, Bishop Rigsby faltered for a moment when he realized he would have to ask one of his parishioners to defend an adulterer, but Mamu shut him up. "Don't be ridiculous. Men are men. They're probably all as guilty of adultery as Josh is."

"The Colsons are going away for the day and want to get an early start." Priddie and Osceola were getting ready to go home. "So I need the truck." It sounded reasonable to me and he promised to be there between five-thirty and six which was when he usually started his workday. That was early enough as far as he was concerned. I figured I had to be on the road before mother left the house so I could park far enough away not to be seen when she turned out of Broadway and started toward town.

That evening, I went up to my room early so I wouldn't have to see her when she came home. I was afraid she might be able to detect something and I'd give myself away. I got into bed and, since I wasn't the least bit tired, picked up my guide to Venice. The first paragraph read,

> The station is about an hour in a gondola
> from the Piazza S. Marco, which is the centre
> of Venetian life. A gondola with one gondolier
> costs 1 lira, each piece of luggage 20 c. extra.

I remember it as clearly as if I had read it yesterday because I must have read it a hundred times trying to force myself to pay attention to two simple sentences, but it was impossible for me to concentrate. From that paragraph on I skimmed, looking at the names of the places of interest all in bold letters—hotels, churches, museums—and reading the odd little notes Mr. Phelan had written in ink that was fading to grayish brown in the margins: *"Tell Grace," "too much salt," "only before three o'clock,"* and *"I am in love,"* which was written two different times. I wanted to know if that meant two different people and if it did, just how long he was in Venice. Of course, he could have been in love with the city itself, or some particular architecture or painting or statue. Like Uncle Josh, I wanted to know everything about John Phelan who stayed at the Hotel Danieli in 1910.

In the early 1950s, when I finally went to Venice for the first time, I used this same little guide, written by Augustus J.C. Hare and St. Clair Baddeley, two names I can never forget. I have been there many times since and I always take it with me. It's like traveling with an agreeable and dependable old friend. Not only is it rich in description of the treasures the city has to offer, but there are also applicable excerpts from the works of Shakespeare, Shelley, Goethe, Byron, and Ruskin, to name but a few. And I like the fact the Messrs. Hare and Baddeley assumed the worldliness of their readers and quoted long passages and bits of poetry in French and Italian, in a book written in English, and never bothered to translate.

When I had had enough of Mr. Phelan and Venice for one night, I put the book aside, turned off the light, and lay staring into the darkness. I knew I wasn't going to sleep. My mind was racing, trying to find other options mother might have had, but the only thing I could come up with was a job that paid more money. And if that were the case, why couldn't she tell us?

It was almost ten o'clock when I heard her come home. She was singing "Shine On Harvest Moon," one of her favorites, as she walked down the path to the porch and entered the house just as she had done so many other nights when she came home. Came home from where? I thought. It must have been two hours later, when I was sure everyone was asleep, that I went down to Estella's room. I couldn't keep my incredible discovery to myself any longer. As quietly as I could, I slipped into her room and gently shook her.

"Estella, don't say anything. It's me."

"Well, who else would it be?" she said in a husky whisper. "What do you want?"

"Come up to my room. I have to tell you something."

"Can't you tell me here?"

"I'm afraid they'll hear us. Come on."

"What time is it, anyway?"

"It's almost midnight."

"Did something happen to Uncle Josh?"

"No, no. Come on, I'll tell you up there."

"This better be good," she said, getting out of bed.

We all had candles in our rooms in case the electricity went off in a storm so I lit mine and put it on the floor next to my bed. This was all very secretive and I thought the electric light would be too much. Estella, still half-asleep, stretched out and I pulled the ladder back up and sat close by so we could talk quietly. Mamu had the ears of a bat. When I told her what happened with the man at the lumberyard she squealed involuntarily.

"Shut up," I said, "they'll hear you."

"My God! I can hardly believe it!" She leaned up on an elbow. "I don't know what to say! Mother! Jesus! Where the hell has she been going every day?"

"I have no idea."

"Honest to God! I think the whole world is going nuts. First Uncle Josh and now mother!"

"I don't know about the whole world, but ours sure as hell is. I'm going to follow her tomorrow morning and see where she goes."

"I want to go with you."

"You can't. If you do Mamu will suspect something. She thinks I'm just going to get Irina."

"How come you get to do everything? It's not fair." She sounded like a four-year-old. But I knew how she felt.

"I'll tell you everything as soon as I get back. I promise."

"Shit," she said. She knew there was no way both of us could go.

"I'm sorry."

She got off the bed, went to the window, and looked up at the moon. "Where can she be going?" She turned to me. "And why didn't Uncle Josh tell us about that woman?"

"I don't know. I guess he felt he couldn't. Probably because she was married. I don't know."

"He loved her all those years. And now she's gone. He'll never see her again. How can he stand it?" She went on without waiting for an answer as she usually did. "Mamu always said he was a little crazy and that's why he lived alone in the shack. That he didn't have any ambition. But I've been thinking about it. It's because he loved her so much and couldn't have her . . . he just turned his back on everything. Yeah, I suppose he is a little crazy. I can understand that, can't you? I mean, imagine if you met the one person in the world you thought was the only person for you and you couldn't have that person." I wondered if she was thinking about Adam. She could have him any time she wanted. "What would you do? I think I'd want to kill myself. Do you think Uncle Josh ever thought about killing himself? I'll bet he did."

I thought about him sitting in the rowboat in the middle of the creek the afternoon I brought him the tray. Maybe I stopped him from drowning himself? More than once, over the years, it has occurred to me that Priddie's sandwich may have saved his life.

I wasn't sure exactly how much of what Uncle Josh told us at the jail Mamu had passed on to Estella and Priddie so I tried to remember everything he said. All about her being a music major and the meetings at the Astor and F. Scott Fitzgerald and how beautiful she was. I tried to make it sound as romantic as I could because I knew Estella would like that. And because she couldn't go with me the following morning, I felt guilty and hoped telling her every-thing I knew would make her feel as though she was included. I was tempted to tell her about Mamu and her loveless marriage, but that could wait for another time.

She started crying and tried to hide it, but I could hear it in her voice. "Just think of him rowing across the lake in the dark and her waiting at the boat house. It kills me to think of them. He really should have told us. It must be wonderful to be able to talk about the person you love. We wouldn't have told anybody and it would have made such a difference for him. It's so sad. Just think how lonely he must have been all these years."

"Yeah, very lonely." I knew what that felt like.

"God," was all she said and went to the door, quietly closing it behind her.

Telling Estella about mother felt very good and I could only imagine how much Uncle Josh must have wanted to talk about Gloria Gardiner.

Chapter IX

There was no sleep for me that night because I was afraid I wouldn't wake up in time to get on the road before mother left the house. I dressed and went downstairs at five-thirty. When I passed the bathroom I could hear her singing to herself as she splashed in the tub and I knew I had plenty of time because her bath and her application of make-up, not to mention fixing her hair, took at least an hour. It had always been a bone of contention in the family. I could smell the richness of the coffee coming up the dark stairwell and I couldn't wait to get a cup. In spite of everything that had happened it was a morning like every other one and it seemed ridiculous. I couldn't get over the feeling that nothing had changed. The constellations should have moved and the sun should have risen in the north for a change. How could the world be so inured to what was happening in my life?

I used the downstairs toilet, washed my face, and ran wet fingers through my hair. Mamu was in the kitchen listening to the radio and cleaning the milk pail, getting ready to go out to the goats. They were already impatiently calling to her.

"You're up early."

"Yeah, well, I couldn't sleep. Anything in the paper this morning?"

"Not about Uncle Josh. It's right there on the table. Looks like England is going to declare war. They don't seem to have a choice, do they? Don't men have anything better to do than fight wars? Honestly! So many innocent people will be killed. Seems like we just had a war." It struck me that Uncle Josh's dilemma was humanizing Mamu. I had never known her to show concern for the human race. She filled a pail with warm water. "Don't you be long getting Irina. Poor thing. She's probably dead from a heart attack being away all night. There's a lot of work to do around here today, so you hurry back."

"What about Uncle Josh?"

"Don't worry about that. I'll take care of everything. I'll be talking to the lawyer today. You just get back here in case we need the truck."

"Yeah."

She went out the door with her pails and clean clothes. "When Estella comes down tell her to collect the eggs. I'm coming," she called to the goats. "Stop making such a fuss."

I turned off the radio, poured myself a cup of coffee, and went out through the mud porch and sat on an old metal lawn chair that Priddie rested in on occasion. The day was as cool and fresh as the first day of creation and there wasn't so much as a wisp of a cloud in the early morning sky. The rain and wind had cleared the air and, for a change, there was no noticeable humidity. It was what Uncle Josh would have called "a Thomas Hardy day" which never made sense to me because the Thomas Hardy he had read to us always seemed bleak and hopeless. Sinclair saw me and snorted a few times as I watched the ducks and geese splashing in puddles that were already drying up. Why they wanted to cover themselves with mud, when they had a perfectly good pond right behind the springhouse, was a mystery to me. I could smell the sweet, old fashioned pink climber on the trellis of the porch, a fragrance I usually took for granted, and I could hear Mamu mumbling her troubles to the goats and the goats contentedly making little snorting sounds in response.

I couldn't get over how ordinary it all was, exactly as it should be, in spite of what I was certain was impending doom. I thought about how painfully contrary life was and wondered how the hell people ever got through it. The sun rose and set and no matter what terrible thing happened, nothing could stop it.

There were times when, as much as I wanted to get away from home and discover what the world was all about, I couldn't imagine being any place else. There were too many compelling arguments to spend the rest of my life exactly where I was. The house and the gabarn, the fields, the creek and the animals, the warmth of the kitchen smells and the feel of fresh laundry, the waxy, clean coolness of the rooms which were off-limits, were all as comfortable as my own skin. I felt I belonged in this strange isolated atmosphere. Estella and I had few friends. We never participated in any extracurricular activities or belonged to any of the clubs at school because we had to be home to work. Since she had graduated she didn't even have the casual acquaintances that I did, the kids I passed in the hall or sat next to in class. As a result, our world had an emotionally impregnable fence around it. It was really all we knew, the only place we were connected, and when I thought about leaving I had an eerie feeling of disloyalty as though I was betraying some intangible entity, the god of home and hearth, that would someday wreak revenge by never letting me come back to stay if I left. I was right.

When Priddie and Osceola arrived a few minutes before six, I was waiting at the front gate, desperate for them to get there before mother came down and I would have to give her a lift into town. I didn't know how I could handle her deception or mine.

"You're like a runner waitin' for the pistol to go off," Osceola said. "You got ants in your britches, that's for damn sure."

"Did you eat some breakfast?" asked Priddie.

"I'm fine," I said as I got in the truck.

"Don't you be too long, boy. I need that truck today. You hear what I'm tellin' you? No Mr. Big Shot driving around showin' off. I know what you kids do. I ain't that old yet."

"I'll be back as soon as I can." I couldn't say I had no idea where and what I would be doing or how long it would take me to do it.

At the end of Broadway I made a right turn and waited in a clump of teasel at the side of the road as far away as I could, hoping mother wouldn't look that way when she made her left turn and headed toward town. My stomach was in a knot and I started sweating in spite of the coolness of the day. I don't think I ever felt so alone in my life.

"*I had a little ball. . . .*" I started singing.

When Estella and I were little and cranky or bored riding in the truck, Osceola sang. His repertoire was limited to two songs. They weren't really songs, just little poems set to a sing-song melody. He called them his Hit Parade musical numbers. They suited his voice perfectly because he couldn't sing worth a damn and he was the first to admit it. The songs were mercifully very short, one having only fourteen words. '*I had a little ball, I stuck it in the wall* (slight pause for dramatic effect) *and that's all.*' And, '*I took my girl a fishin', and sat her on a stump. Along came a bumble-bee and stung her on the dump da da dump dump, da dump.*' Once he started singing Estella and I joined in and there was no shutting us up. We repeated the same little ditties over and over at the top of our lungs all the way to the shore. And if we didn't sleep on the way home, we sang our way back. They became our mantra when we were on the road and were very comforting. That morning, as I sat there, waiting for mother to come down Broadway, watching cars go by, certain that every driver knew I was there to surreptitiously follow her to wherever, I must have sung our little songs a hundred times.

It seemed like hours, but it was only about fifteen minutes before she appeared and turned left on Route 13 and started toward Millersburg. She didn't seem to be in any hurry. In fact, she was dawdling. More like sashaying. That was the only word for it. Almost dancing along the highway to the tune I was certain she was humming. She was wearing a bright yellow and white dress which made it easy for me to see her even when she was quite far away. Waving at passersby and stopping to chat with a few people on the way, she walked slowly along the berm, driving me mad because I was in a hurry to discover where she was going. She stopped to talk to a boy whose older brother, Ted Werfel, was in my class at school, who had a puppy on a leash, which she picked up and cuddled. I had never in my life seen her pay any attention to an animal. An old man, someone she obviously knew, offered her a cigarette, which she declined, shaking his hand before she walked on. She stopped to talk to a woman who was working in her garden and I could see the two of them laughing. This was her morning routine. This was my mother away from the house, someone I didn't know at all. Someone who was comfortable with people I never heard about.

For the rest of my life, every time I saw a woman casually walking down a country road, in Russia, Ireland, Vietnam, Israel, Africa, it didn't matter, I thought of that morning watching my mother. Skin color or costume made no difference. They were all my mother walking Route 13 to Millersburg, part of a continuum, every day, every place in the world on every sun-dappled back road. Even in the most war-torn, godforsaken countries, and eventually I would see many of them, a woman walking alone along a quiet lane gave me great comfort. I suppose it was a reminder of Mamu and Osceola's legacy. The resiliency of the spirit. Life goes on.

There were more cars on the road than I expected that early in the morning. Millersburg was coming to life as mother walked to the bus stop and waited with the other passengers. It was all very social because these were people she had been riding with for years. People with newspapers and lunch boxes and umbrellas, just in case the rain came back. People with someplace other than home to go, who had stories to tell of things that happened since they had last seen each other, who wore new clothes or hair styles that warranted comment and who had husbands and wives and children mother probably knew by name but never mentioned to us. In all those years there had been marriages and births and deaths that mother must have known about, but never discussed at home. She was probably more intricately involved with their lives than she was with ours. She was a stranger to us but a friend to all those strangers. I wondered if I'd like her more if I knew her as they did?

The drive to Laurelwood was endless because the bus stopped at almost every corner and with all that stopping and starting I was afraid the truck was going to overheat. When I passed Colson's Lane I could see it was still a muddy mess and I imagined that I could hear Irina bawling for me to come and get her. Mother got off the bus at the station in the center of town and walked down Emmerson as though she was in a hurry to get wherever it was she was going. I parked the truck on the street and started following her on foot. We walked out of the business district and into the residential, past well kept houses with porches abutting the sidewalk. It was the practical cityscape typical of so many places with colonial roots. There were no little patches of garden, but most of the houses had window boxes that were overgrown and spent with the end of summer. Almost every porch was occupied with someone having morning coffee and watching the traffic. Some said hello and others merely nodded. I smiled and hurried past, hoping I wasn't arousing any suspicions. Mother made a left on Third Street, still walking briskly, and moved into a neighborhood that had a shabby, transitory look and I started to feel uncomfortable. The macadam disappeared and the streets narrowed and became the original cobblestone. There was no longer any semblance of a sidewalk, merely a dirt path that ran along the cobble curb. Occasionally, there was a vacant lot with volunteer hollyhocks and elegant Queen Anne's lace doing their best to brighten a blighted landscape. Here, the streets were less orderly, suddenly turning or circling around, with no sense of direction or plan. I'm sure it was one of the oldest parts of Laurelwood, established back in the heyday of the market when the streets were built to accommodate horse-drawn carts. The further we walked, the more ramshackled the houses became. She turned into a vacant lot and walked along a path until she disappeared behind the houses and I had to run to make sure I wouldn't lose her. The canal ran behind the houses and about fifty feet along there was a narrow bridge which she crossed and walked on down the towpath. We were both out in the open and I was afraid she was going to turn and see me. There were several houses in a small group and finally she stopped in front of one with gray shingles, better tended than most, and fished for something in her purse. By then, I was certain she was going to see me so I fell to the ground and pressed myself as flat as I could. When I looked up she was putting a key in the lock and a moment later she disappeared into the house. Because I didn't know when I'd have the truck again, I didn't have the luxury of indecision so I went to the house, stood for just a moment looking at the clean porch with the newly painted wooden chairs and the pots of yellow marigolds and purple lobelia, and with my heart pounding out of my chest, knocked on the door. A middle-aged man with glasses, a receding hairline, and the start of a gut, answered. He had a scar running from one corner of his mouth, straight down to where it disappeared under his chin. Very much like the slit in a ventriloquist's dummy's mouth. He was obviously startled when he saw me standing there.

"Come in," he said when he recovered. I hadn't said a word. He held the door open and I went into the house.

"Who is it?" called mother as soon as he had closed the door. "Ben! Oh, my Lord!" she said as she came into the room tying an apron around her waist. For a split second I could see her slipping into the giddy, helpless little-girl mode, a knee-jerk reaction in times of stress, but she stopped herself, realizing there was no point to it. "I knew this was going to happen sooner or later." She went to the man and stood very close to him. "Ben, this is your father."

Chapter X

It was well after noon when I returned home. Mamu had called the Colsons several times, wondering what was keeping me. As it turned out, it was impossible to get the truck up their lane and I had to trudge through the mud to get Irina and by the time I led her back to the main road we were both covered with it, having slipped and fallen more than once.

I remember very little after I left my father's house except running to get to the truck because I had been away from home so long. I'm not even sure I paid the stud fee when I picked up Irina. Mrs. Colson chatted on, as usual, but I don't think I heard a word. I do recall driving home, the wind drying the mud on my arms and legs, and wishing Estella had been with me when I met my father because I wanted her to see the man she had idealized all those years. Her handsome, tall, accomplished, artistic, polo-playing bon vivant. The bay rum-smelling, pipe-smoking, well-dressed, perfect man who, in reality, was ordinary beyond description. This was the man who was going to gather the scattered parts of me and make me a whole. Not very likely, I thought.

When I left the highway and turned the truck into Broadway I was armed with information that changed the way I felt about everyone but Estella. Priddie and Osceola were no longer as dependably and exclusively mine as I had imagined. Even my feelings for Uncle Josh were altered. And Mamu didn't survive unscathed. She was the same controlling and demanding tyrant she had always been, only worse.

There was very little explaining to do once Mamu and Osceola saw Irina and me covered with mud. In fact, Mamu was very solicitous, rushing Irina off to the gabarn to bathe her and Osceola took the truck around back to hose off. Luckily, their priorities saved me from having to fabricate a story because by then I was so brain numb I wouldn't have been able to come up with anything very convincing.

Knowing Estella would be chomping at the bit to hear whatever I discovered, I asked Priddie where she was.

"She's out in the fields. Miz Adela sent her to make sure them boys is workin'. You get up stairs and run a bath before you get dirt all over my clean house. You look like you been makin' mud pies."

"I've got to talk to Estella first."

"No you don't. You got to clean up first. You don't know what kind of nasty germs are livin' in that mud. And take those clothes off right now so I can put them to soak."

I knew it was useless arguing with her so I stripped down to my underwear and handed her the clothes.

"Give me the drawers, too. They just as dirty as the outside clothes."

"I'll bring them down after my bath."

"Well, ain't you the modest one! I don't want those dirty things up in my bathroom. Just turn your back. It ain't the first time I seen your bare ass, you know." It was rare and always surprising when Priddie used a crude word and invariably she did it when she thought she was being funny.

I kicked off my underwear and ran naked toward the hallway and stairs.

"Well, ain't you cute," she said, laughing. "It wasn't that long ago I used to powder that little behind of yours. You still just a little boy to me. No matter how much growin' up you do."

"Not any more," I said. Right then I wanted to tell her I knew everything and that I no longer trusted her as unequivocally as I always had, but I thought I should talk to Estella first.

By the end of the day it was humid and sticky again so Priddie left a cold supper for us and she and Osceola went home early. We ate on the side porch in the glow of a citronella candle as a precaution against mosquitoes which Priddie said were fiercer than usual for three days after a storm. The fragrance from the moonflower vine, as heady and sweet as fine perfumed soap, competed with the lemony sharpness of the citronella.

I had told Estella nothing about mother because there was no opportunity to be alone except in passing and I didn't want to start until I could tell her everything. She agonized all through the meal and hardly ate a thing.

"I talked to a lawyer today. His name is Mason. J. Leonard Mason." Mamu took a slice of ham and passed the plate. "I hate that initial business instead of a given name. J. Leonard! Leonard J. is all right but J. Leonard! How pretentious. Well, what can you expect from lawyers. Pass me the deviled eggs, Estella. And why aren't you eating?"

"I'm not very hungry."

"You don't have to be hungry to eat. Put some food on your plate and you'll get hungry. The potato salad is delicious. I like it when Priddie puts the green pepper and cucumber in it."

"What did he say?" I poured iced tea for all of us.

"What did who say?"

"J. Leonard. The pretentious lawyer."

"Well, the news was good. It's about time, don't you think? He said the police probably can't keep Josh in jail. Unless they have evidence or a witness that saw him there the night of the murders they have nothing to connect him to the crime and don't have just cause. They found no evidence, blood, or a weapon or anything like that in his shack. Of course, it took J. Leonard almost the whole morning to say that. That's why they charge by the hour, you know."

"When will we find out?" I asked.

"J. Leonard is coming down to Laurelwood tomorrow. His offices are in New York. He's a big shot lawyer from what Alice's husband says." For whatever reason, Mamu refused to call Rev. Rigsby, *bishop*. In fact, she never referred to him as anything but "Alice's husband." "I'm going to meet him at the courthouse. Pass me the tomatoes."

"I'll drive you," said Estella, jumping in before I could say anything.

"Fine. Now put some food on your plate and eat. You're not a child anymore, you shouldn't have to be told when to eat. Honestly!"

It was Estella who came up with a plan so we could be alone. When we had finished our dessert she said, "Want to see if we can get some frogs tonight, Ben?" She turned to Mamu. "You'd like some frogs' legs, wouldn't you?"

"I don't like you out on the creek at night. It's different when Josh is with you. And what if that murderer is around? What if, just for the sake of argument, it wasn't that Gardiner fellow. You know, the husband. What if it was some other maniac?"

"Are we grown up or not?" I said. "One minute you tell us we're adults and the next you treat us like kids. And you know as well as I do that Gardiner did it. You're just using that as an excuse to keep us here."

"Well, go then. I don't give a fig one way or the other. Why would I want to keep you here? I want you to go. Then I'll have a little peace and quiet. Go on. I'll clean up and make a plate for your mother. Who knows when she'll be home?"

Estella and I changed clothes and got the lantern and started along the path to Uncle Josh's shack, ostensibly to get the rowboat. About halfway there she said, "Damn it, tell me. Mamu can't hear us. I'm about ready to explode."

"O K. Are you ready for this? She looks after none other than Devlin Whyte every day."

"Who is Devlin Whyte? Oh, my God! Oh, my God!" She jumped up and down a few times and then started walking in little circles.

"He's alive? Oh, my God! I don't believe it." I wasn't sure if she was laughing or crying. "Did you see him? Did you meet him?"

"Come on. We'll go down to the dock "

"Stop being so damn mysterious. Jesus, you drive me crazy."

"I don't want to leave anything out. I want to organize everything that happened today in my mind."

"Wait a minute. Why does she have to look after him? Is he sick or a cripple or what?"

"No, he's not sick. Just wait a few minutes and I'll tell you everything."

"I hate you."

"Come on," I said as I started along the path.

"One thing. Do we look anything like him?"

"Well, not really . . . except maybe the eyes. His aren't blue, but they're shaped like ours. And his nose is like ours."

"What color are his eyes?"

"Green, I think. Or hazel. I know they're not blue or brown. I'm sure of that."

When we were settled on the dock I started from the beginning, from the time I followed mother into town to the bus station. Estella listened, but was obviously interested in getting to the part about our father even though she didn't interrupt until I described the house on the canal.

"It sounds awful. Is it like slums? I didn't know Laurelwood had any slums. Why do they live there?"

"It's all they can afford. He has to give her the money to bring home every week. You know, her salary from the lumber yard."

"What was the house like?"

"Better than most along there. It's kind of nice being right on the canal. There were a lot of people fishing along the towpath. A lot of colored people with their bamboo poles. . . ."

"I don't give a damn about the people fishing! What was the house like?"

"Inside was clean and neat. Believe it or not, mother's a good housekeeper. The furniture is old, but the living room has nice wallpaper and there are pictures on the wall. There are pictures of us all over the place. Mother made me breakfast."

"You ate with them?"

"Yeah. The first few minutes were awkward. Worse than awkward. I was . . . well, I don't know exactly what I was . . . mad . . . hurt . . . I don't know."

"You sat down and had breakfast with our father! My God! What did he say? What did you say? Mother just said sit down and I'll make breakfast? She never does that here."

"She's different with him. She's like a different woman. She's a lot like . . . well . . . remember the night we danced with our shadows? You know, the night she got the job at the lumberyard and we went out to catch the night crawlers? The night of the shadow rebellion when we all kept dancing even though Mamu told us to stop. Remember what she was like that night? Cool and confident, leaning out of the bathroom window and laughing? All of that little girl shit aside. Well, that's what she's like when she's away from here. Not just with our father, either. I watched her walking along the road and at the bus stop, confident and casual, talking and laughing with people. You'd never know her, Estella, I swear to God you wouldn't. Away from Mamu she's another person. She even looks younger and prettier."

"So, you walked up to the door and knocked and she said it was our father and then what? Oh, God, I can't believe this."

I tried to remember everything exactly the way it happened.

"I didn't want you to find out like this," said mother after she introduced me to my father. "I wanted to tell you. Honestly, I did."

This was confounding at first and I felt embarrassed for them and for me. I felt like I had caught them doing something I shouldn't see. In a flash I could see them naked and sweaty, sliding all over each other, panting and squealing, and it was revolting. I remembered when

I heard about Uncle Josh and Gloria, thinking about the two of them making love, and it was so different. They were in the boathouse, just as Estella had pictured them, their bodies as white as statues in the moonlight and when I imagined them holding each other, him inside of her and she with her legs wrapped around him, it was exciting. But mother with this stranger was sickening. I started for the door.

"Ben, don't go. Let us explain. For Christ's sake, give us a break." Then, as a moral reminder he added, "We were never divorced, you know. If that's what's got you upset."

"What do you mean, if that's what's got me upset? Are you crazy? Don't you think I might have reason to be upset?"

"I'm sorry. That was stupid. But I wanted you to know we've always been married."

"Well, that makes everything all right, doesn't it."

Mother got between the door and me. "Ben, I beg you. You can't go like this. Please, give us ten minutes. Is that too much to ask?"

"Why didn't you tell us, mother?"

"I wanted to. I did. But I was waiting for the right time."

"And when was the right time going to be.? How long has it been? Two years?"

"I know how you must feel." My father took a step toward me and I moved away. I was terrified that he might touch me.

"Get away from me. You don't know how I feel! How could you? You don't even know me. How could you know how I feel?" My eyes started stinging and I was afraid I was going to cry. "You haven't seen me in fifteen years. I just had my seventeenth birthday. Thanks for the card. Oh, that's right. I didn't get a card. Of course, I've never gotten a card." I wanted to punch him in the face.

"Your father picked out the cat's eye ring."

"Really! Well, that makes up for the last fifteen years, doesn't it?" I took the ring off and threw it at him. "Here, I don't want it anymore."

"Ben, stop it," said mother as she retrieved the ring from the floor. "He's your father."

"No, he's not. He's nothing to me. Nothing."

"I deserve that. I know I do." He took a deep breath and let all the air out of his lungs. "What do you want me to say? I'm sorry. I know that isn't enough, but I am sorry."

There was so much I wanted to say to him. When he was just the memory with the pipe it was easy to venerate him. There was always the possibility that he was dead and therefore unable to come back to us and that made him mythic and oddly heroic. Death can be so ennobling. He could be all the things Estella said he was and the very idea of him provoked a kind of reverence. But there he was in the flesh, alive and apologetic, smelling of cigarettes and sweat, balding and pale and pathetic. I wanted to accuse and berate him and tell him that he was to blame for everything that went wrong or ever would go wrong in my life. More than anything, I wanted to hurt him.

"Weren't you even curious about Estella and me? We're your damn children! Didn't you want to know what we looked like?"

"I've always known what you looked like. Your mother sent me pictures all the time you were growing up. Just look around this place. And you both waited on me at the vegetable stand. Several times."

Estella erupted. "I waited on him? Why didn't he say something? God damn everybody! Did you recognize him when he opened the door?"

"No. I mean, how many people have we waited on? I don't remember what most of them look like unless they're regulars."

"Mother sent him pictures? Where? Where the hell was he all that time?"

Mother had never been out of touch with him even though, after he left the house, he moved all over the country going from one job to another. From what they told me that morning, he was a maverick, not quite the dreamer tripping over his dreams that Uncle Josh had described. He worked on oil rigs in Texas and shrimp boats in Louisiana; he picked cherries in Oregon, and worked on a hog farm in Iowa. To hear him talk there wasn't any place he hadn't been or anything he hadn't done. They wrote to each other weekly, mother receiving her letters care of the Flowers who smuggled them to her when they came to the house. Both Priddie and Osceola knew my mother had quit the lumberyard and was keeping house for my father. And so did Uncle Josh. Only Mamu, Estella, and I were ignorant of their relationship and, mother assured me, as far as Estella and I were concerned, it was only because we were young and predisposed to loyalty to Mamu.

"We'll always be children to them, you know that? We're only grown up when it suits their purpose. God, I hate them all. Everybody knew but us. Priddie never said anything. Neither did Osceola. I can't believe they would do that. Every time we asked about him they knew where he was and never said anything." She got up and paced the dock before sitting down again. "Did they all know about Uncle Josh and Gloria Gardiner? I'll bet they did."

"I asked mother and she said they didn't. I believe her. She said she was as shocked as we were."

Estella swung the lantern down over the creek and there was a shift in light and shadow, almost as if the earth was rearranging itself. We could see minnows in the shallows breaking the surface of the water, sending tiny circles colliding with one another. Neither Estella nor I said anything for awhile. I had had the whole day to think about mother and Devlin Whyte but it was all new to her and there was so much to digest. she was obviously in a turmoil sorting it out. I had no idea what she was thinking but I suspected that, like me, her initial reaction was unforgiving rage. With the lull in the conversation I became aware of the babble of the crickets and tree frogs and the cicadas, but instead of being comforting and almost mesmerizing, as they usually were, the chatter was irritating.

"We're outsiders in this family, you know that? What do we know about anybody?" She turned to me. "God, I don't even know you, Ben. And you don't know me, do you?"

That was true. Estella and I didn't know each other. We lived in the same house, ate meals together, worked together and even swam unashamedly naked together, but we didn't know each other. We rarely talked and had no idea what each other wanted or expected from life. Whatever little kinship we had was the result of a united front against Mamu and mother. Maybe that's all siblings are supposed to have, but I wanted more. It was hardly the foundation for a solid and lasting relationship. I don't know if I had ever loved Estella as a sister because until that time she had been little more than a casual friend. But as ashamed as I was to admit it even to myself, she was a sexual fantasy. She and Uncle Josh.

"Well, I know a lot more about our parents." I didn't want to answer any questions she might ask in an effort to finally get to know one another. It wasn't the right time. If there would ever be a right time. But the circumstance of our parents finally being together, the shared secret, was lending itself to a kind of intimacy. I could feel it starting and it made me uneasy. I changed the subject. "Do you remember Mrs. Amberhurst?"

"Yes, of course." Her mood changed. "She was my first grade teacher. She had a bun on top of her head and the start of a mustache. She was always laughing and she stuck pencils in her bun. I liked her. She was one of my favorites."

"I had her in first grade, too. And so did our mother and father. Do you believe that? They met the first day of the first grade at Millersburg Public. Mrs. Amberhurst arranged the class alphabetically and he sat right behind her in the last row. They talked about it as if it were yesterday. He said that was when he fell in love with her. Mother cried most of the day and wet her pants because she was afraid to ask to go to the lavatory, but it didn't matter to him. That night at the dinner table he told his parents he had met the girl he was going to marry. Estella, you should hear them talk about it. Laughing and crying and filling in the details for one another. It's amazing. There was mother with a man I had never seen before and they knew everything about each other. Did you know that his father, our grandfather Whyte, was the mayor of Millersburg? When they were kids in school. Why didn't anyone ever mention that? He was an insurance salesman."

Estella had tears in her eyes. "They met in the first grade? And mother never told us any of this. God, I feel so cheated."

Everything they told me came tumbling out. How my grandfather Wayland wanted to send mother to Miss Goodman's Academy for Young Ladies, but Mamu said she wasn't bright enough to be anything more than an average student and the academy would be a waste of money. As it turned out, it was one of the few things for which mother was thankful to Mamu. Had she gone to the academy she might never have met my father. When they were in high school, Mamu wouldn't let mother go to the school dances with him. She wouldn't let her go to the dances at all.

"Well, we never went to any dances, either. None of that has changed. I didn't care, but I'm sure mother did."

"Mamu hated Devlin Whyte. No question about that."

"Why did she hate him so much?"

"You know her. Does she need a reason? She doesn't like anybody."

"How did she ever get to marry father?" said Estella.

"I don't want to call him father." It rankled me to say the word. "I don't think of him as my father. He's just Devlin Whyte. A man mother's married to."

"OK. How did she ever get to marry Devlin Whyte? Is that any better?"

"She got pregnant. With you. On purpose."

It was the first time Estella heard that she was conceived out of wedlock. She was astounded. "No!"

"When he came out of the army, he asked mother to marry him."

I told Estella about the long scar on his face where he was wounded and I could tell by her reaction that she was still holding on to pieces of the glamorous father she had imagined all those years. The army, the wound, and getting mother pregnant only served to make him more romantic.

"She got pregnant before she was married? On purpose? I can't imagine her ever having the courage to do that."

"I told you, she's a different person when she's with him."

When he came back from France he went to work in the insurance business with his father and failed miserably. He went from one job to another, but he never lasted very long at any of them. As far as Mamu was concerned he was a good-for-nothing, but mother was pregnant and refused to have an abortion so they were married.

"Mamu wanted to have me aborted! My God, I'm sure Priddie and Osceola know all about that, too. Damn, that makes me mad. If Mamu had her way, I wouldn't be here."

"Well, neither would I. They might never have gotten married."

But they *were* married, in a quick and embarrassing little service on the side porch of the house. The only people in attendance were Mamu, Devlin's parents, and his brother who was a witness and a justice of the peace, a complete stranger to all of them, who performed the ceremony. Grandfather Wayland couldn't be there because he had to stay in town on business. There was no celebration of any kind. No flowers, no photos, and no wedding cake. When the service was over Mamu sent everyone home and made it clear that as soon as the baby was born her intention was for them to get divorced. They lived on the third floor in what was to become my room and Mamu made life miserable for both of them. Grandfather Wayland wasn't around enough to care one way or the other. He had a woman, or women, mother wasn't sure, in New York and spent most nights away from Millersburg. Mother said she couldn't remember a single conversation between Mamu and grandfather. They had stopped communicating before she was born.

Devlin managed to stay in the house four and a half years in spite of the seismic build-up of tension that made life miserable for everyone. There was nothing he could do that suited Mamu. Finally, in a ridiculous showdown over how much butter he put on his toast, Mamu threw him out of the house.

"You think we've had it bad; well, it's been a picnic compared to them."

"Why didn't we go with him? How could he leave his wife and children behind?"

"Money. He didn't have any. What were they supposed to do with two babies and no money? I'm not trying to make excuses for him, but I kind of understand. And mother couldn't leave because Mamu threatened to cut her out of the will. Don't forget, there was still a lot of Wayland family money back then."

"I wouldn't care about the money if my husband had to leave. I'd go with him and I think she should have, too."

We didn't talk for awhile. She went to the end of the dock and sat by herself.

"How tall is he?"

"About as tall as me. I might be a few inches taller."

"Does he smoke?"

"Cigarettes."

"Does he drink?"

"I don't know. It was breakfast."

"What did you have?"

"Scrambled eggs and sausage. And toast."

"What does he do? For a living I mean."

"He works at the penicillin plant over in Hockney."

"Doing what?"

"I don't know exactly."

"Is he nice to mother?"

"I think so. Seems to be, anyway."

"What does he call her?"

"Eulalie. Sometimes, 'Euey'. Sometimes, Honey."

"What does she call him?"

"Dev or sweetheart."

"Did you see them kiss?"

"No. He held her hand, though."

There was silence again and I thought of something I hadn't told her. "We have a half-sister someplace in Pennsylvania."

"We do? Jesus! Does he see her? Or is it the same as it is with us? I think I'm starting to hate him."

"No, he doesn't see her. The woman married and her husband adopted the baby."

"God, we have a sister!" She didn't say anything for a few minutes. "He probably has babies all over the place."

"He said it was the only time he cheated on mother."

"He said! And she believes him? She is stupid."

"Well, it's more like she *wants* to believe him."

Another silence. "Did you like him?" she asked.

"I don't know." I had to think about it a moment. At first I hated him, but after they told me what their lives had been like I wasn't sure.

Estella came back and sat next to me. The lantern was losing its brightness because the wick needed to be trimmed and the chimney was getting black.

"I keep expecting Uncle Josh to come out of the shack," she said and took my hand. It was as casual as though she always did it. My initial reaction was to pull away because it made me very uncomfortable, but I fought the impulse and we sat holding hands, listening to the sounds of the night.

"What's going to happen next?" she asked.

"Mother's going to leave. Now that we know, there doesn't seem to be any reason for her to stay here."

"She'll be able to spend the whole night with him."

"She's going to talk to you about it. Then, she's going to tell Mamu."

"How do you think she'll take it?" Estella sounded tired, as if the weight of knowing was too much for her and had beaten her down. She sounded like a tired child fighting sleep.

"She'll tell her to go. You know she will. She probably won't say much else."

"Makes me feel sick just thinking about it."

"I know what you mean. I think she's going to leave in the next few days."

"It'll be strange when she goes, don't you think?"

"I don't know. I don't think it will make much difference."

She thought about it for awhile. "You're right. It probably won't make any difference at all." She leaned her head on my shoulder for a moment, then kissed me on the cheek. I looked at her and when I did, she kissed me lightly on the lips. I had never kissed anyone on the lips before and was shocked to feel how soft and yet electrifying the kiss was. She pulled away and looked at me as though she was trying to decide what to do next and then we kissed again, mouths open, our tongues probing. It only lasted seconds, but every part of me responded. When she pulled away she said, "I want to do that with Adam. I love him."

"I know you do."

"Come on." She picked up the lantern and started for the house and we never said another word.

Chapter XI

Mother moved out of the house the same day Uncle Josh came home. She was gone before he arrived.

J. Leonard Mason was right when he said the police didn't have sufficient evidence to hold him. Apparently, the provincial lawmen of Laurelwood were no match for big-city J. Leonard. Estella and I both wanted to go and pick up Uncle Josh but, as usual, there was work to be done and since it had taken me so long to bring Irina home Mamu didn't trust us, so Osceola took the truck and waited at the courthouse for his release. Mamu wouldn't go along because after only one meeting with Mr. Mason she couldn't stand him. By the time he and the police sorted through all the red tape it was late afternoon when Osceola and Uncle Josh got back to Broadway Acres.

The night before, mother came home earlier than usual. I don't know if her timing was good or bad, but we were just finishing dinner on the porch, in the middle of a heated argument, when she came walking down the lane. Priddie and Osceola had gone for the night. The talk at the table had been mostly about Uncle Josh coming home and I could tell by the way Mamu was criticizing everything he had done that whatever compassion she may have felt for him while he was in jail was quickly disintegrating.

"It's time things got back to normal around here," she said pouring herself coffee. "Not that it ever will after what he's done. He is such a fool! I hope, after what's happened, you can see him for the fool he is." She wanted confrontation and she wasn't getting it, so she was obviously disappointed.

"I'll clear the table," said Estella, getting up.

"No, you won't. It's rude to start clearing the table before everyone is finished. I'm not finished."

"You do it all the time," I said knowing I was taking my life in my hands.

"Why are you so argumentative, Ben? Why must you always take your uncle's side?"

"I didn't say anything about him."

"Mamu, please. . . ." said Estella.

"Sit down."

"I'm feeling a little sick."

"You sound like your mother. Are you going to faint, too? I thought you were above that nonsense, Estella. Stop it right now and sit down."

She sat, eyes averted, and started playing with the salt and pepper shakers.

"I've made a decision and I want to tell you both what it is. I know you won't agree with me but after what's happened, when all this settles down, if it ever does, I think your Uncle Josh should leave."

"Leave!" Estella sat up straight in the chair, knocking over the salt shaker. "Why? He hasn't done anything. He didn't kill those people. Why should he leave?"

Mamu's mouth stretched into a hard thin line. "He carried on with a married woman." She said it with more ferocity than she would have had she accused him of the murders. "He's weak and he has no moral fiber. He's disgusting. He's disgraced us all."

"I don't feel disgraced. No one knows anything about it." I was giving her the argument she wanted.

"The whole town will know it sooner or later. All of this mess will come out publicly. And not only here in Millersburg. There were two murders, for heaven's sake. Two murders that made international news. If you don't think the details of every involvement the victims had will make the papers then you are just plain stupid. I know better than that. We've worked too hard to make this business a success. . . ."

"You can't just abandon him after what he's been through."

"This is your brother, for God's sake," said Estella. "And where would he go? He's always lived here."

"You two have such misplaced loyalties."

It was then that mother came down the walk and up on the porch. Estella and I knew she was going to confront Mamu. I was already feeling sick and I could see Estella cringe.

"I could hear the three of you halfway down the lane." It was obvious she had prepared herself for this, and the little-girl act was nowhere to be seen, even though she was nervous and visibly shaking.

"You're home early," said Mamu without looking at her.

"Is all this ruckus about me?" asked mother. Her voice was thin and strained.

"Why in the world would it be about you?" Mamu put her coffee cup down. "Why you?"

Mother turned to me. "You haven't said anything?"

"I told Estella. . . ."

Mother touched her cheek. "I'm sorry. I wanted to say something. I hope someday you'll be able to forgive me."

"You told her what?" Mamu was insistent. "What's going on here?"

Mother looked at Mamu for a moment before smiling and saying, "Devlin just dropped me off at the end of the lane." Mamu went white. "I'm leaving tomorrow. I'm going to live with my husband."

Mamu's face tightened and her eyes narrowed. I had seen that happen so many times, whenever things weren't exactly the way she wanted them. After several seconds, all she said was, "Good."

"He's coming to pick me up in the morning."

Mamu thought about it a moment, then turned to me. "You knew this?"

"Yes."

"I see."

Mother had decided what she was going to say and when she did speak up it sounded almost like a recitation. "You once told me my children didn't need me. Well, as much as I hate to admit it, you were right." She was still shaking, trying to get control of her voice. "They needed you to take care of them and you did. I'm grateful for that. I truly am and will always be. Anyway, for whatever reason, I thought I should be here . . ."

"And now you don't think it's necessary for you to be here, is that it?"

"They're not children, they certainly don't need me. And I don't want to pretend anymore."

"And just what are you pretending?"

"Everything, mother! Good Lord, how can you ask that? But it doesn't matter." She turned to Estella. "Can I talk to you alone? Would you come up and help me pack?"

"She'll be there after she's helped me clear the table and do the dishes."

"Whenever," said mother, and started to leave.

"Just where are you going to live with your husband? Am I allowed to ask any questions?"

"Of course. Ask whatever you like. I'm moving in with him in Laurelwood. Actually, I've been living with him for more than two years. Well, almost living with him. We had breakfast and dinner together and a good part of every evening. I kept house for him."

"How touching. You kept house for him."

"I've loved every minute of it."

"So, you've been lying to us for two years. You weren't at the lumberyard. You're a liar, Eulalie."

"Yes, I am. I'm a liar."

Mamu snorted. "What a ridiculous woman you are. You've always been intolerably ridiculous."

"I certainly have. Simpering, weak, and, as you say, ridiculous. Always playing the fool. I was exactly the way you wanted me to be. It was how I survived. Stupidity was my only defense. It was a way of getting attention. Irritation is better than nothing at all. You'll never have any idea how mortifying it was. Anything to please you, Mamu. Anything. I have you to thank for whatever I became." Her voice was stronger, more in control.

"It's like you not to take responsibility for yourself. To blame your shortcomings on someone else. I wouldn't expect anything different."

"I'm curious about something, mother. I won't ask if you ever loved me. I know better. But, did you ever like me? Simply like me? I'm really curious."

Mamu looked at mother for a moment and then looked away. She was uncomfortable. "The day you were born some idiot midwife, fat and sweaty and all smiles, put you in my arms and I looked at you and . . . and I felt nothing." She was admitting something even she found difficult to talk about. "The truth is I tried. I really tried, but I had no idea how to do it. Mothers are supposed to love their children. It's automatic. Or at least it's supposed to be. I know that. I tried, but I couldn't."

"How can you say that about your own child?" Estella's romantic dream was love, marriage, and babies. It was beyond her comprehension how any mother could not love her baby. "My God, Mamu, she was yours. Your tiny little baby."

"You weren't a very likable child, Eulalie. And you looked exactly like your father. By the time you were born I hated him. If you must know, I didn't want a child. I never wanted one. You were a mistake. You wanted the truth."

"Yes. Thank you for that." Her shaking had stopped, and she stood there, smiling at Mamu. "It all makes sense. None of this hurts me one little bit." She was obviously lying. "Nothing you can say can be anywhere near as painful as what I've imagined all these years . . . wondering what I had done that was so wrong. And my only sin was looking like my father. How unforgivable of me!"

"I did the best I could." Mamu stood up and started clearing the table. "If you're leaving in the morning have your bags packed and on the porch. I don't want that man in my house."

"Fine." Mother started once more to go into the house. "You make leaving very easy," she said over her shoulder.

Mamu stopped what she was doing. "You can simply walk away from your children?" There was a bit of maneuvering in the question, an attempt to make mother feel guilty about leaving.

"Ben knows where we live. They're welcome any time they want to visit. Or any time they want to stay."

"You'll be back," said Mamu. "Knowing your *husband,*" she made it a filthy word, "you'll be back."

"No, mother, I won't. Not in a million years." She went in, closing the screen door behind her. "Estella," she called, "whenever you're free." She stood behind the screen for a moment. "There's one more thing, Mamu. Something I was afraid to tell you, but now I'm not. I'm pregnant. And I want this baby more than you could ever imagine." She walked down the hall.

"She's pregnant," Estella said to me. "That's wonderful." That was something they hadn't told me but it didn't come as any great surprise.

Estella took a stack of dishes and started for the kitchen. "Mamu, how could you say those things?" she said as she went.

Mamu stared at me, doing her best to make me feel uncomfortable, before asking, "You know where they live? Have you been there?"

Without answering I got up from the table, crossed the porch, and went down the path to the gabarn.

"Don't walk away from me when I talk to you." But I could hear the slightest hint of defeat in her voice and I felt that somehow, even though mother did the fighting, we had all won a battle. The granite hold Mamu had on us had started to chip away because of the things she had said to mother and she knew it.

Sinclair whinnied at me and I stopped to rub the velvet of his nose, and the goats made little grumbles of annoyance because I wasn't paying attention to them. They came out of their shed and stood with their front feet on the fence, stretching their necks so I could pet them. I moved along the path down to the creek where I sat on the dock in cool white moonlight. I could hear fish jumping and something, probably a raccoon, splashing somewhere along the bank. I thought of Mamu admitting that she had never liked mother and using the word "mistake." I vomited into the creek. Beads of sweat broke out on my forehead as I lay there retching. When the violent convulsing stopped I went down a path that led to the bank. I stripped off my clothes and waded out into the water until I was up to my chin, taking great mouthfuls to rinse the sour taste out of my mouth. The water was cool and cleansing and I let myself sink beneath the surface and drift along with the current while I thought about opening my mouth and filling my lungs with water. It almost seemed like the obvious and only thing to do. I had once read an account of a man who had drowned and been revived and all he could remember was hearing music just before he lost consciousness. Mozart? Liszt? Louis Armstrong? I wondered what music I'd hear. But I couldn't do it and instead, burst through the surface, gulping for air. How long I floated downstream, I wasn't sure, but before I knew it I was almost to the place where the creek widened before emptying into the lake which was two miles from our dock. I could see the lights of the first houses at lakeside and the silhouettes of people standing on the bridge spanning the end of the creek. I swam to the bank and sat there for some time before walking back to the shack through the brush and tree roots and fern. Brambles tore at me, but I hardly felt them, even though I could see rivulets of dark blood on my legs. When I got back to the dock, I stood shivering in the moonlight as an owl flew by, its great wings as silent as falling snow. I went into the shack, lit the oil lamp, cranked up the Victrola, decided to listen to Chopin. *Andante Spianato* and *Grand Polonaise, Op. 22*. Uncle Josh called it thinking music. After turning off the lamp, feeling empty and cold, I crawled into his bed. There was still the smell of him on the sheets and there was some comfort in that. If he was going to leave, I was going to leave. I wanted to get away, so far away I'd never be able to find my way back. I wanted to erase every memory I had and start all over again. I wanted to cry, to feel the great release I had always felt as a child when I cried myself to sleep, but something had changed and I knew the luxury of tears would be a rare option. It was the inevitable compromise growing up demanded. The scratches made me aware of my body and I threw the sheet off to see if there was still bleeding, but it had stopped. Looking down at my nakedness, so pale and ghostly in the moonlight, as pale and ghostly as I had imagined Uncle Josh and Gloria Gardiner at the boathouse, my body became the body of a stranger and there was something exciting about it. I touched my face, my lips, and I thought about Estella and our kiss. I rubbed the stubble on my chin and ran my hands down my neck and over my chest, lingering on my nipples. I started getting hard and I moved slowly down to my navel and felt the little line of hair that led down to the thicket, and when I took hold of myself, although it was something I had done countless times before, it all seemed new and exhilarating. There had always been closed doors, the fear of discovery, and a rush to get it over with. But I was lying there with the door and window open to the night. It was all so new and free I could have been touching someone else. Friction and fantasy. Mother was young, soft, pale thighs open, receptive, and inviting and Devlin was thin and sinewy, the scar on his face only a few years old, still red and angry, blood pulsating, he was on her and in her, back arching, pumping hard to create a baby so they could always be together. Halves of the perfect whole. Then, there was Estella, Adam, and Uncle Josh, all naked and glistening, one starting where the other left off, touching, kissing, lips and tongue searching, all interwoven and compliant. And there was me. The stranger who couldn't cry. Someone who needed and wanted to be touched, with no guilt and no shame, giving and available. Friction and fantasy.

When I finished, spent and sweaty, I thought of absolutely nothing and went into a deep, satisfying sleep.

It was almost eight when I got to the house the next morning and mother was waiting on the porch, bags packed and anxious to go. Estella and Priddie were with her, but Mamu was nowhere to be seen. Osceola had gone into Laurelwood to fetch Uncle Josh.

Estella came to me when she saw me crossing the lawn.

"Where's Mamu?" I asked.

"In the sewing room. She milked the goats, took her coffee, went upstairs, and closed the door. She hasn't said anything to anyone. Not even to Priddie. What happened to you last night?"

"I stayed in the shack. Did you talk to mother?"

"For hours. It was good." She touched my arm and I could almost feel the tension and anticipation. "I'm nervous about meeting him. I don't know what to say."

When we got to the porch Priddie came down the steps. "I'm goin' to fix you some breakfast. Sounds like everybody around here worked up an appetite last night." She almost whispered, afraid Mamu might be listening. Then she leaned in close and said, "You goin' to have a little brother or sister. How about that!"

"Yeah, how about that."

"Come on, I'll fix you some waffles. You love waffles."

"No, I don't want anything."

"You got to eat somethin'. Keep your strength up." Food was the great cure-all to Priddie. She led me up onto the porch as though I were an invalid. "I'm just glad it's all out in the open. Terrible burden keepin' a secret like that. Lord almighty." I looked deep into her yellow eyes, wondering if she knew how betrayed I felt. "Don't go lookin' at me like that, Ben. I did what had to be done. Sometimes a child needs to be protected from things. Bad things and good things.

That's just the way it is. So don't you go blamin' Osceola and me. We did what we thought was right."

"I didn't say anything, did I?"

"Lord, don't you think I know what's goin' on in your mind? Don't ever imagine that you foolin' me one little bit 'cause that's a big mistake."

"Morning, Ben," said mother. "Estella and I had a nice talk, didn't we?" She didn't wait for an answer. "You didn't come home last night. We were worried. Are you all right?"

"Yeah, I'm OK."

"May I ask where you were?"

"No. It doesn't matter." I hadn't forgiven the lie she had been living for the past two years but, having seen her stand up to Mamu the night before, my anger was diminishing.

Just then, Devlin whipped up a cloud of dust coming down Broadway, causing a rumpus with the animals. He parked the faded old blue Ford sedan in front of the house and even before he got out Estella started down the path. They met at the gate and after only a moment's hesitation went into each other's arms. I wondered if Mamu was watching from behind the lace curtains in the sewing room window.

Estella's acceptance of him and disregard for any transgressions disappointed me and I felt I had lost an ally. It was a terrible, empty, isolating feeling. I didn't want to talk to him, or even look at him for that matter so I went into the house to the kitchen to get coffee. Mother followed.

"Here," she said and held out the cat's eye ring. "We're not as bad as you think we are. Maybe someday you'll know that. People do things to survive. And keeping secrets isn't the worst of them. Please, take the ring. I'm sure you like it. You don't know it now, but one day it will mean something special to you. Believe me."

I hesitated a moment, then took it and slipped it on my finger.

"It looks nice." She touched the stone, smiled, and left.

The morning paper was open and there was an article headlined, "Bodies Released To Families." The coroner's office had released the bodies of Gloria Gardiner and Marius Dorfman. He was to be flown to Germany where there would be a memorial service held in the Cathedral of Ulm, his hometown, and interment in the family plot. A celebration of his life and contribution to the world of music was planned at the Metropolitan Opera House in New York. There were no details given for plans for Gloria Gardiner's funeral except that it would be a private service in Pittsburgh, for family members only. How unfair, I thought, that Uncle Josh wouldn't be there to pay his last respects, but her murderer would. I didn't want Uncle Josh to see the paper when he came home so I tore it up and put it in the trash.

Years later I was in Germany, driving from Stuttgart to see a friend, a writer who lived in Augsburg, and I went through Ulm, famous as the birthplace of Albert Einstein and the burial place of Field Marshal Erwin Rommel. I thought about Marius Dorfman so I stopped to visit the cathedral. The second largest Gothic church in Germany, it has one of the tallest church towers in the world. While I was there I decided to look for his grave and when I found it the headstone was overdone yet impressive, decorated with angels and musical notes, obviously marking the final resting place of a very important man. I asked an elderly man walking his dog where I might find Rommel's grave. That was in the early fifties and, if Dorfman's grave was ostentatious, the grave of Rommel, the brilliant and well-respected Desert Fox, was marked by an almost embarrassingly unobtrusive little stone.

I took some coffee, went into the hall, and stood back from the screen door watching Estella and Devlin. They seemed as comfortable as two people who had always been part of each other's lives. Mother and Priddie had joined them and were loading bags into the car. She was leaving the house, never to return, but it seemed like an ordinary family scene, everyone laughing and chatting, almost as though she and Devlin were going on a trip and Priddie and Estella were seeing them off. It was what it should have been for the past fourteen years and I couldn't stand there and watch.

I went into the back yard, on through the tomato fields, and joined Janos and Stash harvesting cantaloupes. It was unconscious and robotic, what I did every day without thinking, as automatic as breathing. I wanted to keep going, to get the hell away from the tight little world in which I lived. Almost everything that happened in my life happened right here and I was trapped. It was stifling. But I didn't know where to go.

As always, the boys were speaking Hungarian, having their own private jokes and making each other laugh, probably at my expense even though I knew they generally liked me.

"Hello, Ben," said Stash. "You want cigarette?" He was broad-shouldered and beefy, and although he joked with Janos, there was a serious side to him. Janos, on the other hand, was wiry and animated, almost incapable of standing still or saying two words without laughing. They were both older than I was, in their early twenties, yet I always referred to them as the "boys."

Everything seemed wrong. Mother was leaving and Devlin, like it or not, was back in our lives, providing Estella with the father she always wanted even though he was a far cry from the one she had imagined. But flesh and blood was tangible and so much better than the fabricated ideal. He certainly wasn't what I wanted. Uncle Josh was coming home, grief-stricken and humiliated, and Mamu was going to tell him to leave. She would make life miserable for all of us, including Priddie and Osceola, because mother stood up to her and because there had been a conspiracy against her. But Janos and Stash were smoking, the melons were ripening on the vine and had to be picked. Everything had changed, and nothing had changed.

Chapter XII

The next few days were tense, like waiting for a time bomb to explode. Was Mamu, as threatened, going to tell Uncle Josh to leave and, if so, when? Osceola had several heated arguments with her which Estella and I only heard in bits and pieces when he confronted her one afternoon in the gabarn.

"There ain't no reason to send that man away."

". . . my decision, not yours."

"You live to regret it. You wait and see."

". . . not your business."

"Like hell it ain't."

". . . worked too hard for what we have. I'll not stand by and watch it all fall apart."

"Ain't nothing goin' to fall apart if we don't let it. What is wrong with you, woman? And just in case you didn't notice while it was all happenin' he worked just as hard as we did. This here is his place, too."

". . . for his keep. That's what he worked for. Nothing more. If it was up to you, we'd give part of the business to the Hungarians?"

"Yeah, I would. That Stash is a hard-workin' man. I don't understand you! How mean can one little woman be?"

"You have no idea." Mamu headed for the house. The discussion was over.

Meals were torturous because she barely spoke and Estella and I were limited in the topics of conversation. Whatever we really wanted to talk about, Uncle Josh or Mother or Devlin, was out of the question. There was never even any mention of mother's departure. One day she was there and the next she was gone, like my childhood conception of death when death and disappearance were interchangeable. It was more like she had never existed. Certainly, as far as Mamu was concerned, mother had crossed the line when she decided to leave and she was never to be forgiven. Sadly, Estella and I were right when we said her leaving would make very little difference in our lives.

The *Reminder* occasionally reported on the investigation of the murders, but it said little more than that the police were on the job and had promising leads. Of course, what the leads were was never mentioned. Claude Gardiner was apparently still not a suspect. But we couldn't even discuss the murders because that would have led to talking about Uncle Josh.

His return was a mixture of joy and sadness. We were happy to have him at home, but he was so lost in his grief he was hardly there. Again, we were limited in what we had to talk about with him. There was certainly no mention of the murders or his time spent in jail. It was decided, by Osceola, that we would wait for him to broach the subject. Priddie was teary-eyed every time she looked at him, but she never said anything when he was around. We did everything we could to try to make him feel better but, as Priddie said, "Maybe he'll never get over it. It's the second time he lost that woman. How many people in one lifetime have to mourn the same person twice? It's a wonder he ain't dead hisself. How can a body stand it? Lord Almighty."

"You know what we ain't done since the beginnin' of summer?" Osceola was trying to think of something to shore up his spirits. "We ain't been to the ocean. It wouldn't hurt to have some good fish for a change. Maybe we go and see old Eddie Ninetoes. You think that's a good idea? You think we can get Mr. Josh away from his shack if we ask him to go fishin'?"

He appreciated the offer, but wasn't interested. Nothing interested him. Estella told him all about mother and Devlin, many, many times, trying to get him involved in a conversation, but about the best he could do was smile and say he was happy they were finally together. He stayed in his shack or sat on the dock watching the creek flow by, but he never took the boat out, and rarely came to the house.

"You think he has plans to do something to himself?" asked Estella.

"No, that never crossed my mind but now that you said it I'm sure I *will* think about it." She and I, without planning it, almost took turns spending time at the shack so Uncle Josh wouldn't "do anything."

Priddie was fixing all his favorite foods, but he wouldn't come to the house. I think he was avoiding Mamu and I couldn't blame him. He was mortified for having spent time in jail and for the exposure of his affair with Gloria Gardiner and he probably sensed that Mamu was going to ask him to leave. Estella and I brought his meals to him, but he ate little more than enough to survive and was visibly wasting away. We thought he was dying.

"Nobody dies of a broken heart," said Priddie after we told her. "Least that's what folks say. I don't know if I believe it or not. Seems as good a reason to die as any other, don't it?"

Finally, after several weeks, it was Osceola who pulled him back into life. He went down to the shack, something he rarely did, and confronted Uncle Josh. Quite simply he told him that grief was one thing and we all respected his grief, but it was autumn and that meant everything had to be harvested, every hand was needed to get the work done. If food was Priddie's cure-all, work was Osceola's. It was the first time Uncle Josh truly responded to anyone. He started working that day and work stimulated his appetite, and he started eating. But he still didn't come up to the house for dinner.

One morning, after things had settled back into our old routine, I came down earlier than usual, before Priddie and Osceola arrived and before Estella got up. Mamu had finished the milking and was straining the milk before putting it in the springhouse. The coffee was perking and there was a loaf of bread on the cutting board waiting to be sliced. It was a gray day with the chance of rain and the kitchen was dark and gloomy.

"Morning," I said as I flipped the light switch.

"We don't need the lights on this time of day." She didn't turn to me. "The electric company gets enough of our money."

"OK." I switched the lights off. "Looks like it might rain."

"Maybe. We could use it."

"Yeah, I guess we could." Having dealt with the weather, the conversation seemed to end as she went about her business without saying anything more. I felt awkward because I hadn't been alone with her since the night on the porch after mother announced she was leaving when I refused to answer her and went to the shack. The silence was unnerving. "No radio this morning? You're really saving on electricity, aren't you?"

"Don't be funny. The news is all bad and I don't want to listen to it. Germany and Poland . . . and England and France . . . of course they don't seem to have any choice. It's terrible. Nothing but war. I'm sick of it." She turned and looked at me. "Why are you up so early?"

"Couldn't sleep. And I'm hungry."

"Slice the bread if you want toast. That'll hold you until Priddie gets here. You might have to sharpen the bread knife."

I sliced the heel off and the knife cut through quickly and cleanly. "The knife's fine. You want some toast?"

"I'll get it when I come back from the spring house." She was cool, but at least she was talking to me. "I'll have two slices." She went out the door with the pail of milk carefully covered with cheesecloth so the flies couldn't get to it while the cream was rising. I sliced four pieces of bread, put two on the toast rack on the stove, turned on the gas, and got the butter and strawberry jam out of the icebox.

When she came back we had breakfast together. What little conversation there was was concerned with the goats, the "boys," the harvest, but nothing about anything that was really pertinent to what was happening in our lives. I knew there were things she must have wanted to ask me about mother and Devlin and I would gladly have told her but I didn't know how to bring up the subject. Finally, when even the small talk trickled down to nothing, I blurted it out.

"They live in a house on the canal." She stopped eating, toast between the plate and her mouth, but didn't say anything. "It's an old house, but they have it fixed up nice."

"Nicely."

"Nicely." I told her how I found out about mother not working at the lumberyard and how I followed her the day I picked up Irina from the Colsons'. I told her everything and I had a great feeling of relief.

"Why didn't you tell me this before?"

"I couldn't."

"Priddie and Osceola knew, didn't they?"

"Yeah, they did."

She shook her head knowingly. "What do you think of your father?"

I had to be careful with my answer. She was looking for an ally. "He's not what I thought he'd be."

"I'll bet he isn't!"

"I don't mean there's anything wrong with him. . . ."

"What do you know!"

"Mamu, did you ever think that maybe you expect too much from people? Did you ever think of that?"

"I don't expect anything from men." I hadn't specifically said men. "Nothing! Good God. I expect too much! If that doesn't take the cake! I know better than that. I learned not to expect anything a long time ago. My father married a girl young enough to be his daughter. That's right, Josh's mother was younger than I was. And she was my stepmother!"

"I knew that."

"Did you know my mother hadn't been dead six months when he married her? I never told you that part, did I? Mother wasn't even cold in her grave. Jenny was a patient of his. He was probably carrying on with her when mother was still alive. Makes me sick to think about it. You should have known your great-grandmother. She was a wonderful woman, smart and kind. And sick all those years. You never would have known it, though. She was an angel. You would have liked her, Ben." I had never seen this Mamu. She had never talked about her mother, but remembering her softened not only her voice, but also her face. For a moment she was transfigured, then the hardness returned. "And poor, stupid Jenny. I guess she was a nice enough girl. I never knew her. I didn't want to spend any time around my father. I couldn't stand to look at him. He buried Jenny, too, you know. Flu. She died of flu when Josh was a child." I had already heard most of what she was telling me. "And Josh!" She shook her head. "What a poor excuse for a man he is."

"Don't start on Uncle Josh."

She turned to me. "Don't you give me any arguments. I know how you feel about him, but he's a waste of time. Why don't you wise up and see him for what he is? So, he was disappointed in love. So what! A lot of people are disappointed in love, but they don't go and hide in a shack for the rest of their lives doing nothing. The real crime is, he's got a good head on his shoulders. He could have been anything he wanted, but he didn't want anything except feeling sorry for himself. That's what he does best. Well, *I* don't feel sorry for him. He has no gumption. What has he ever contributed? Answer me that! As far as I'm concerned he is a lazy good-for-nothing and I will regret taking him in until the day I die."

She took a sip of her coffee and in the lull I wanted to defend Uncle Josh, but there was no point.

"Then, to take up with that woman after all those years. She was married. She had a husband and child, for heaven's sake, but that didn't matter to him. Not as long as he had what he wanted. Sex! It's all they think of. It disgusts me. He disgusts me. Sneaking around at night. You don't sneak around if you know what you're doing is right. You can quote me on that. And this business with the police. It was downright mortifying. People like us don't go to police stations. I had never even been inside a police station until that day and I have him to thank for that."

"He didn't commit the murders." I had to say something.

"He might just as well have. It was because of him that those two people are dead. If he hadn't carried on with that woman her husband wouldn't. . . ."

"You can't blame him for the murders."

"Well, he's as much to blame as anyone. He had to have that woman. Just like your father and mother. Now there's a man to be proud of! Did you know he got your mother pregnant before they were married?"

"Yes, they told me."

"They did?" She was surprised. "A fine mess that was. If it hadn't happened she never would have married him, I can tell you that much."

"They told me they did it on purpose. So they'd have to get married, you'd have to let them marry."

Mamu had to think about that for a moment. "I wouldn't put it past them. Then, she got what she deserved. And now she's pregnant again. At her age. It's obscene. I pity that child. What kind of life will it have? I don't think he ever had a job that lasted more than two weeks. You want to talk about a good-for-nothing!"

"He's got a job now. At the penicillin plant in Hockney."

"What's penicillin?"

"It's some new kind of medicine."

"Probably snake oil if your father has anything to do with it."

"I didn't know my grandfather Whyte was the mayor of Millersburg."

"That's all your father has to brag about, is it?" She smiled. "His father the mayor. Well, he was a scoundrel . . . a crooked politician . . . no better than your father. It's bad blood, that's what it is. That insurance company of his robbed half the people in town. I heard *he* was carrying on with some woman, too."

It started to rain one of those soft, misty kinds of rain and Mamu went to the window over the sink and looked out. "The boys will use this as an excuse not to come to work. One drop of rain and they don't show up. You'd think they were made of maple sugar. Talk about worthless."

And then I asked the question that I had wanted to ask for so long. I knew I'd never have a better opportunity.

"What happened to grandfather?"

"Your grandfather Wayland?"

"Did you kill him?"

"Of course not."

"I don't believe you." I had never said anything like that to her before. "I'm sorry, but I don't believe you."

She chuckled and said, "No, I didn't kill your grandfather. How gullible you are, Ben. Gullibility is the curse of the honest man. Or is it stupidity. Maybe both. Really! I wish I *had* killed him, but I didn't do it. You want the truth. All right. I'll tell you what happened." She turned to me and, leaning on the sink, continued. "There was a woman . . . Charlotte Campbell . . . your grandfather knew her before we met. She was older than Bayard by only a few years and she was married to a real estate man. Well-respected. He bought and sold half of Manhattan. Well, your grandfather and Charlotte Campbell had an affair. As I say, this was before he met me. It was a scandal, and when his parents found out they gave him an ultimatum, stop seeing her, marry, and settle down or he would be disinherited. His mother had a long list of eligible young women, but out of spite he looked for someone he knew she wouldn't approve of. Me. He married me to spite his parents. That's the truth. I'm not imagining it because he told me." She nodded her head a few times for emphasis. "I say I only married him because I knew he could look after me. You know what I mean. The Wayland money, but that's not true. By the time we were married there was a lot more to it than that. He was a charming man, your grandfather, no doubt about that. How well do you remember him?"

"I remember him, but he was never really here. I do remember when he drove us to the shore to meet those friends of his. Mother got carsick. And you wanted to drive. But I was only six when he disappeared."

"Only a few weeks after we came back from that ridiculous honeymoon he started seeing her again. He said he had to stay over in the city on business. Well, foolish as I was, I believed him. He would stay in New York a week at a time and I was left to take care of the house. Priddie only came in once or twice a week in those days so I was by myself most of the time. There was no business to look after, nothing to do except tend to the house and wonder what my husband was up to. When I got pregnant he stayed away more and more. I don't know when I started to put two and two together, but when I confronted him and told him I thought he was seeing another woman, he admitted everything. He told me all about the beautiful Charlotte Campbell, and how much he loved her and what a terrible marriage she was in. So, when your Uncle Josh sat there weeping in the jail about his lost love and her bad marriage . . . well, it was old news to me. I had heard it all before."

Mamu came back to the table and sat down. It had to have been mother's leaving that affected Mamu enough to tell me all this. I'm sure she realized her hold on the family wasn't as strong as she had thought it was and maybe she was trying to explain herself. Or, perhaps she was just telling me why she hated men. I've thought about that morning so many times over the years.

"He told me he intended to go on seeing Charlotte and there was nothing I could do about it. If I wanted a divorce he'd agree to it. It was up to me. He was very pleasant about it. Of course, your grandfather was always pleasant. Everybody loved him. I thought about it long and hard and I didn't know what to do. I couldn't stand to be in the same room with my father and I would have died before I asked him for anything. And, don't forget, I was pregnant. Well, by then I had become comfortable in this house. It was my home and I liked it very much. Still do. So, your grandfather and I had a business arrangement. He would provide everything I needed and, at the time of his death, our child and I would inherit his estate. For all intents and purposes we had a marriage, but really, it was a business deal. His life was in New York and mine was here in Millersburg." She folded her hands on the table like a good little girl in school. "Pour me another cup of coffee, Ben."

I got the pot and filled both our cups.

"Now, what I'm about to tell you must never go any further. You must tell no one. Not Estella, your mother . . . no one. Ever. You promise?"

"Yeah, I promise." I sat down, feeling very nervous about what-ever she was going to say.

"The night your grandfather died he came down from New York a couple of hours after dinner. I remember because I had done the dishes and you and Estella had gone to bed, and your mother was reading you a story. I heard the Phaeton come down Broadway and wondered what he was doing home in the middle of the week. I went out on the porch and he was standing there, all smiles, his usual charming self. "Come on, Adela, I want to take you for a ride," he said. I wasn't interested. "I have to tell you something. Come on. One little ride, is that so much to ask?" I knew it wasn't about Charlotte because she had died a few years before that. A boating accident on Long Island Sound. This was 1929, don't forget. I think by the time she died they had stopped seeing each other and there was a new woman. Anyway, I agreed to go with him just to find out what was on his mind. So I went upstairs to tell your mother but found her asleep with you and Estella. It was a cool night so I stopped in my room and got a heavy white sweater to throw around my shoulders and went down and got in the car. When we pulled out of Broadway he turned left and we headed for the shore. I don't think there was much conversation, but if there was, I don't remember any of it. I guess I thought he would tell me whenever he got around to it. He was very playful that way, always had little games. After we had been driving for about an hour, he pulled off the highway and drove through the pine barrens on zig-zagging, winding little dirt trails. Finally, at the edge of a small lake he stopped the car, rolled down the window, and lit a cigar.

"Is it too cold for you with the window open?"

"No, I'm fine. What is this all about?"

"I don't know if this little lake has a name or not," he said. "I used to come camping here when I was a boy. I had two friends whose families had houses on Miller Lake, Lionel Greshon and John Day. Lionel wore a special shoe because one leg was a half-inch shorter than the other. He was the best swimmer I ever knew. And John, well, he was about the smartest kid I ever knew. Skinny as a whippet and smart as hell. He and I served together in the Philippines. We named this lake the Lake of the Spirits because it was so eerie back in here. We made up all kinds of fantastical ghost stories sitting by our campfire at night, stories about the spirits that haunted the lake. Scary as hell." He took a mouthful of smoke and slowly blew it out between his pursed lips. "I loved it here because nobody ever came around. We never saw a single person. We always pretended we discovered it. And maybe we did? Who the hell knows? When you swim in there are skeletons of dead trees on the bottom. And eels all over the place, they only made it creepier. And there are a couple of old cars down there, too. We used to hold our breath and sit in the driver's seat. I loved camping down here. It was like the end of the world." I hadn't said a word and he sat there smoking and smiling as he remembered the good old days. He took a few more puffs on his cigar. "We're broke, Adela. Dead broke. It's my fault. I played the market and invested everything in worthless stock. Everything's gone. There's nothing else to say. I'm sorry."

"There's nothing left?" I asked. "How is that possible?"

"Nothing but the house and the car. That's it. I'm sorry," he repeated. "I'm sorry about a lot of things and I apologize."

"It's a little late for that, isn't it. You brought me all the way down here to tell me that? You could have told me on the porch and turned around and gone back to New York. Let's go home."

"No, I don't think so. That's your home, not mine." And he reached under the seat, pulled out a revolver, and without saying another word put it to his temple and pulled the trigger."

"My God, Mamu, what did you do?"

"I sat there horrified, not believing he had killed himself. It was preposterous. For a moment I even thought he was playing some kind of terrible joke on me, but I saw the blood and I started screaming so hard my throat hurt. Then I retrieved the lit cigar, which had fallen between his legs and threw it over his slumped body, out the window. There was surprisingly little blood. Some on my sweater and dress and some on the seat. His head was on the steering wheel and he was staring past me with a look of surprise in his eyes. I will always remember that almost innocent look of surprise. That was the last time I ever looked at his face. Peculiar that it would be so childlike and . . . well, innocent is the only word I can think of. I sat there wondering what to do next. And then I started to get angry. Really angry. If he wanted to kill himself that was fine, but why involve me? Did he think there was something noble in blowing his brains out and wanted to make sure I was there to see it? As far as I was concerned there was nothing at all noble about it. It was downright contemptuous. How he must have hated me to do such a dreadful thing. I reached over, opened the door, and pushed as hard as I could until his body tumbled out of the car. I think I was screaming at him all the time. He crashed down on the ground and I can remember the sound of twigs cracking when he hit. I sat there horrified at what I had done, thinking he'd suddenly get up and stand at the window, accusingly, with blood running from his forehead. It was very frightening, I can tell you that much. I got out of the car, the bravest thing I've ever done, walked around to the driver's side, stepped over him, and got in. I was shaking so much I could hardly turn the key in the ignition. Then, without looking back, without giving a fig for what happened to his body, hoping that animals would come in the night and rip him apart and buzzards would pick over him the next day, I drove down the winding little roads for what seemed an eternity, hoping I'd find the highway and once I did I headed for home."

I just sat there, stunned and dumbfounded.

"I parked the car and got a bucket of water and washed the blood off the seat. All of it didn't come out. If you look closely you can still see dark shadows after all these years. I tried to wash the blood out of my dress and sweater but the stains were set so I burned them. I had to burn my shoes, too. Had I been able to dispose of the car I would have. Instead, I decided it would stay in the garage and never see the light of day. So, I locked it up and there it sits." She played with the crusts of toast on her plate. "I was certain someone would find the body. I was feeling guilty, almost as though I had killed him, and wondering how I was going to explain how the car got in the garage. Your mother was still asleep so I didn't have to worry about her. About a week later, when his office called several times looking for him, I reported him missing and when the police came to the house I just said he had left the car there and nobody said anything more about it. The weeks turned into months and the months into years and all the time I waited for his body to be found. Finally, well, you remember when his skeleton was discovered, all I can say is it was a great relief. I didn't have to live with wondering what happened to his remains. Yes, I was glad to know they found what was left of him, but I'll be damned if I was going to go to the cemetery and honor him. I'd rather have shot myself."

I heard the truck pulling in behind the house.

"Priddie and Osceola are here. Remember, Ben, not a word of this to anyone. Not a word."

"I promise." It was such an astonishing revelation I couldn't face anyone so I decided to say I had a headache and was going back to my room for awhile.

"A headache? So early in the mornin'? Never heard of such a thing. You ain't never had a headache in your whole life far as I know. You sick?" Priddie was heading for her herbs, ready to look after me.

"No, not sick. It's only a headache. I think I'll just lie down for a little."

"I'll bring you a cup of sage tea. That'll fix you up real good." She put the kettle on the stove. "I just hope you ain't comin' down with somethin'. Too early for the flu."

"We'll talk later, Ben." Mamu knew I had to be alone to think things over. But we never had the opportunity to talk about grandfather again.

For the next few days Mamu and I had a covenant. She honored me by telling me something she had never told another soul and because of that I wasn't even tempted to divulge her secret to anyone. As a result of the telling everyone seemed to relax even though they knew nothing about it. It was because Mamu changed. She had finally, after all those years, told someone her dark secret. Suddenly, there didn't seem to be any threat to Uncle Josh staying with us. She even went out of her way to ask him to come to the house for dinner. I hoped it might be because I accused her of expecting too much of people. The next afternoon, the day after she told me about grandfather, she asked Osceola where Uncle Josh was working and when he told her she walked out into the fields to talk to him. The sun was blazing and Mamu, who did as much of her outside work before and after the heat of the day, took an umbrella to protect herself. It was the first conversation they had had since he came home from jail. He was harvesting eggplant and, although we couldn't hear what they were saying, we saw him stop dead when she approached him. They looked like they could have been modeling for one of the bucolic impressionists, or maybe Millet or Corot, she with her umbrella and he with a purple eggplant in each hand in the middle of a ripening field. Even the light was right. The deep yellow of an early autumn sun. They only spoke for a few minutes and when she started back toward the house we could see, quite clearly, his whole body relax. That night, dressed in his finest, he came to dinner. Priddie was so delighted she cooked a meal worthy of a holiday. Her wonderful fried chicken, potatoes roasted with garlic and rosemary, corn on the cob, coleslaw, sweet and sour cucumbers, buttermilk biscuits, and peach shortcake with fresh whipped cream. And she went all out with the table dressing. The Sèvres china, the silver with the mother-of-pearl handles, the damask linen, and Waterford crystal, with candles flanking a bouquet of roses. She didn't care whether it might annoy Mamu and Mamu had the good sense not to say a word. It was one of the most unforgettable meals we ever had and not just because the menu was so outstanding. Because Uncle Josh had finally come home it was more memorable than any Christmas or Thanksgiving. Also because it was the last meal we had together. The next day all hell broke loose.

Chapter XIII

The incessant ringing of the phone awakened me and when I opened my eyes it was still dark. I turned on the light and looked at my watch. It was just before five in the morning.

"Is somebody going to get that?" called Mamu. "Estella, go down and answer that phone. Who can be calling at this hour? It can only be trouble."

I put my pants on and ran down the stairs, passing Mamu on the landing. "Did Estella already get it?" I asked. "It stopped ringing."

"I suppose she did. She's down there." Mamu was in her night-gown with her long grayish red braid hanging down her back and her favorite old chenille robe thrown around her shoulders. "I can't imagine who that could be. It's not civilized to call at this hour! Maybe it's your mother. I wouldn't be a bit surprised if they were in some kind of trouble. Didn't I say she'd be back?" She sounded hopeful.

Estella was on the phone. "Oh, no," she said. "Oh, my God."

"Who is it," I asked.

She covered the mouthpiece and said, "Osceola. You won't believe what's happened." She went back to talking to him. "Uh huh . . . uh huh . . . well, I don't know. I don't know what to tell her . . . Oh, God, this is terrible . . . But how can they do that? . . . Oh . . . All right.

No, we won't let anyone in. . . . OK, we'll see you then." She hung up the receiver.

"What was that about?" I turned on the hall light.

"Who was that?" called Mamu.

"Osceola. There's trouble. There's a piece in the Laurelwood paper about Uncle Josh being held by the police for questioning."

"That's all we need," said Mamu. "That is *all* we need." She went into her bedroom and slammed the door.

Estella pulled me down the hall away from the stairwell. "That's not the worst of it. A man in Osceola and Priddie's church works for the *Laurelwood Register* and he brought a copy of this morning's paper to the Flowers. Oh, my God. It's unbelievable."

"What is it? Jesus!"

"There's an article about Uncle Josh and there's a picture of the three of us swimming in the creek."

"Naked?"

"Of course, naked. When did we ever wear swimsuits? Osceola said not to say anything to Mamu about the picture until he gets here. He also said there'll be reporters as soon as the sun comes up. He and Priddie are just leaving the house. He phoned to tell us not to talk to anybody from any papers if they call."

"They can't print pictures of naked people in the paper."

"I asked how they could do that and he said there are little black rectangles covering just enough to keep it decent. Who could have taken a picture?"

"How the hell do I know. Shit! I wonder if you can really see it's us." The phone rang and I grabbed it before it could ring a second time. "Hello?"

"It's not my fault," it took me a moment to recognize Margaret Breedlove's voice. She was crying so much I could hardly make out what she was saying. "He promised he wasn't a reporter. He came up and started talking to me at the diner. I was having the ham loaf special. A very nice young fellow . . . His name is Hare . . . Oh, I don't know what to do. I asked if he was with the press and he said no. I swear he did. I'm going to lose my job, I just know I will. I didn't mean to do anything to hurt your uncle. I swear. We were just talking. He promised me it wouldn't go any further than the diner. He had the ham loaf, too."

"Who is it, now?" called Mamu.

"Go back to bed. I'll tell you about it later." I whispered to Estella, "It's Margaret."

"How can I go back to bed? Use your head." There was a hard edge to Mamu's voice. "It's time for me to get up, anyway. I'm getting dressed." Her bedroom door slammed again.

"What did you tell him, Margaret?"

She wasn't interested in answering me. "Sheriff Anderson is mad as hell. Some crazy person woke him up hollering at him for letting a murderer run around loose in Millersburg. The paper makes him sound crazy. Your uncle, I mean! Not the sheriff. Sort of hints that he could possibly be the killer. Well, the sheriff just gave me hell. Why'd he think I did it in the first place, that's what I'd like to know. I told him I had no idea that fellow was a reporter. He's going to fire me, I just know he is." And she started blubbering again.

"Where did the picture come from?" I asked. Estella had her ear to the receiver with me.

"That wasn't from me. I swear to God I never gave him a picture, Ben. I swear on my mother's grave. I'd never give anybody a picture of all of you with no clothes on. Where would I get it? But I know who did give it to him. They were in here trying to get money from Sheriff Anderson for some pictures, but he said he wouldn't touch them with a ten-foot pole. Say what you will about the sheriff, but he's an honorable man. He said those pictures were nobody's damn business. Really what he said was 'goddamn business' but I don't like to swear."

"Well, who was it?"

"Those McElway brothers. They're just as dumb as dirt. They don't have one brain between the two of them. They make me sick."

"The rotten McElways" were paying us back for usurping what they thought were their exclusive rights to trap muskrat along the creek. Stealing our traps wasn't enough. We hadn't even set them for years. They were as tenacious as pit bulls when it came to getting revenge.

"Those bastards, " said Estella.

"They must have been spying on you from the creek bank when you were swimming. Anyway, that's what Sheriff Anderson said when they showed him the pictures. Can you imagine? They wanted money. I guess they don't have anything better to do. They ought to try getting a job, then they might mind their own business. That's what I said to the sheriff. Let me tell you something, though, there's nothing to be embarrassed about. You all look real nice naked. I wish I looked that good. And the pictures are decent, don't worry about that. Those little black flags cover all your goodies. Actually, it's kind of hard to tell who it is in the picture. It's taken from a long way away and it's kind of grainy, you know what I mean?"

I hung up the phone.

"What are we going to do? Mamu will kill us." Estella went into the kitchen and turned on the light.

"Well, if you can't really see it's us. . . ."

"What difference does that make? If the paper says it's us and there's a picture there. . . ."

"We'll have to wait and see it."

"It's us. You know it's us."

"I'm going to get dressed." I went down the hall and started up the stairs when Mamu came out of her room.

"What is going on? Calling people this early in the morning! What did the piece in the paper say?"

The phone started ringing.

"Estella, don't talk to anybody." I yelled down to her. "Answer it, then hang up and then, take the receiver off the hook. Osceola said not to talk to anybody."

"Are you going to tell me what the paper says?" Mamu took my arm and turned me to her.

"I have to get dressed. Osceola's on his way. He's got the paper with him. I don't really know what it says. You can read it when he gets here." Mamu's door was open and the ceiling lit up from the headlights of a car coming down Broadway and the geese and guinea fowl started making a ruckus. I knew it couldn't be the Flowers. It took longer to get to us from town no matter how fast Osceola was driving. "Oh, shit!"

"You watch your language."

"Estella, lock the door. Whoever it is don't let them in. I'll be down as soon as I get shoes and a shirt on."

"I would like to know what's going on." She was pushing the last of the hairpins into her bun as she started down the stairs.

When I was dressed and came down, only a few minutes later, Mamu and Estella were standing at the open front door talking to a dark-haired young man who didn't look that much older than me.

"I told you not to open the door," I said.

"I opened the door." Mamu glowered at me. " I guess I can open the door in my own house."

"My name is Thomas. Carl Thomas. I'm with the *Reminder*. Why'd you give the story to the *Laurelwood Register* instead of us? Why'd you do that?"

"We didn't give the story to anyone," said Estella.

"I'd like to talk to Joshua Pritchard."

"He's not here. Do you know what time it is? What the hell's wrong with you? We don't have anything to say. To you or anyone else." I started to close the door.

"Well, I have plenty to say," said Mamu. "And I'll start by telling you to get off my property. Right now, or I'll call the police."

"You're the girl in the picture, aren't you?" he said to Estella. "And you're the other guy. What do you have to say about the picture?"

"Nothing. Get away from here." I pushed the door closed and locked it.

"What picture is he talking about?" asked Mamu.

"Wait until Osceola gets here."

"I'll make some coffee," said Estella.

"What are you afraid to tell me? There is something you're afraid to tell me, isn't there?"

"Mamu, why don't you go and take care of the goats. Osceola will be here by the time you finish the milking."

"You're getting pretty bossy, aren't you?"

She was out in the gabarn when Osceola and Priddie arrived. Estella and I read the piece quickly in hopes we'd find something to use in our defense once Mamu got her hands on it. Just as Margaret said, the photo had been taken from a good distance and our faces weren't at all discernible. But the text named us and there was no mistaking our dock and the *Santa Maria*. And, unfortunately, he mentioned Broadway Acres several times. The article was written by Lyle Hare, Margaret's nice young man from the diner with the ham loaf, and went on to tell about Uncle Josh being held by the police in Laurelwood because he had been a possible suspect. There was evidence of an alleged relationship of a sexual nature with the deceased Mrs. Gardiner, but not enough evidence linking him to the murders to hold him in custody. He was being represented by J. Leonard Mason of the law firm of Bernstein, Mason and Brewer of New York City. Uncle Josh was portrayed as an eccentric recluse, a very handsome eccentric recluse who looked somewhat like Tyrone Power. The words were right out of Margaret's mouth. He was also, quite possibly a vegetarian and a Buddhist, certainly a socialist and a nudist, the proof of which being the accompanying photo, taken by an unnamed source, of Mr. Pritchard swimming with his niece and nephew, Stella and Ben Whyte. He left the "E" off Estella's name, which was something she couldn't abide. He went on to say there was a possible connection between Uncle Josh and the German *Nacht Kulture,* a holistic approach to healthy living that started in Germany after World War I which espoused exercise, diet, meditation, and nudism. The fact that Hitler and Germany were in the news made our dips in the creek suddenly sound sinister, almost as though, along with everything else, Uncle Josh was un-American. Just to round things out there was a subtle implication of possible incest. Why else would the three of us, brother and sister, uncle and niece and nephew, be swimming naked in the creek? Since my sexual fantasies sometimes included Estella and Uncle Josh I could feel myself blushing when I read the incest part.

"How long you been swimmin' together in your birthday suits?" Priddie was merely asking a question. There wasn't the slightest hint of accusation in her voice.

"We always did," said Estella, looking up from the paper. "Is this guy crazy? Where does he get this vegetarianism and Buddhism stuff?" That obviously seemed more peculiar than the implication of incest. "And is Uncle Josh a socialist? Unbelievable!"

"I think we're about to see the start of another world war soon as that screen door opens and you-know-who walks in." Osceola sat at the table and held his head in his hands. "We're in for some big trouble, I can tell you that much. And poor Mr. Josh, I wouldn't want to be in his shoes."

"Maybe we can hide the paper and keep her from seein' it?" It was the first time I ever heard Priddie suggest anything even slightly dishonest.

"She's goin' to find out about it sooner or later. Hide it! What's wrong with you, woman? It'll be on the damn radio, you know it will."

Mamu came into the kitchen without her milk pail. She was so anxious to see the paper she stopped milking, something she had never done.

"Let's see what the fuss is all about." She sat at the table and read the article. Estella and I stood near the sink waiting for her reaction. When she finished she sat looking at us without saying anything.

"Now, don't you go flyin' off the handle. . . ."

"This doesn't concern you," she said without looking at Osceola.

"Doesn't concern me! What the hell are you talkin' about? Since when does whatever happens to them two not concern me? You just tell me that."

"This is between me and my grandchildren. It might be better if you and Priddie went outside."

"It ain't such a bad thing," he said. "Lord amighty, lots of folks swim naked. It's supposed to be healthy."

"Adam and Eve didn't have no clothes on." Priddie was clutching at straws, however ridiculous, searching for some way to defend us.

"Outside, please."

"Don't you be hard on them children, Miz Adela. They didn't do nothin' so terrible. Lord knows we all can imagine what we got under our clothes so why's everybody make such a big fuss about being naked? Evil is in the person that looks for it. That's what my Aunt Moll used to say. So if you see evil here that means you got to question yourself." Priddie opened the screen door. "Just think about that."

"One thing, Osceola." It was the first time Mamu took her eyes off us and looked at him. "I want you to go down to the shack and tell Josh to be off this property today. Tell him to pack up his things and get away from here."

"He can't do that. Long as the investigation goes on the police says he got to stay here."

"Then let him go and stay at the police station. I never want to see him again. If he isn't gone today I'll call the police and have him arrested for the corruption of minors."

"You can't do that," I said.

"He didn't corrupt nobody." Osceola stood his ground in the doorway. "Jesus Lord!"

"I will call the police and have him put back in jail. And take my word for it, that's not an idle threat."

"Well, I ain't going down and tell him. No, ma'am. You do your own dirty work. Come on, Priddie. I don't like it in here. Let's go out where we can get some fresh air."

When they were gone Mamu came to us, her face red with rage. I had never seen her so angry.

"What do you have to say for yourselves?"

"It wasn't anything to get upset about. You're making too much of this." I thought minimization might be the best approach.

"Did he ever touch you?" she asked Estella.

"No. Of course he didn't touch me. Mamu. . . ."

"I don't believe you."

"He didn't. God!"

"What about you?" she turned to me.

"No. Never. It wasn't like that. The reporter is making up all that stuff. Did you ever know him to be a vegetarian?"

"Or a Buddhist?" added Estella.

"All we did was swim naked. It was nothing more than that. It wasn't such a terrible thing."

"It is a terrible thing. It's not normal. He talked you into it, didn't he. I mean swimming without your bathing suits. Have you no shame at all?"

"Nobody talked anybody into anything." I suddenly felt she had no right to tell me whether I could or could not swim however I wanted. "We just did it, that's all. And, no, I didn't have any shame. And I don't now."

"Estella, how could you?"

"Mamu, we started doing it when we were kids. A lot of kids swim without any clothes. It just seemed natural for us".

"Well, it's not. A grown man running around naked with children. It's not natural at all."

"I never thought about it. And there was no one there to see us." Estella looked at me. "At least we thought there was no one."

"If there was nothing to be ashamed of, why didn't you tell me?"

"Because we knew this is exactly the way you'd react. Uncle Josh said. . . ."

"So, he told you not to say anything."

"No, he didn't. But we all know how upset you get. This is ridiculous." I didn't feel defensive, merely angry. "No matter what we say it isn't going to make any difference. You're never going to understand because you don't want to. This is a waste of time. So why don't we just save our breath and end the conversation. You believe what you want to believe. But I'm telling you, nothing happened."

"The two of you make me sick to my stomach. I have no respect for either one of you."

"I'm sure you don't. But then, you never did."

"What's that supposed to mean?"

"'Do this, Ben. Do that, Estella. Sit. Stay. Work. Sleep.' Where's the respect in any of that? That's how you've treated us all our lives."

"Ben, don't." It was getting to be too much for Estella.

"Well, I'm sorry if I didn't treat you properly. Just remember if it wasn't for me, nobody would have taken care of you. Certainly not your mother and father."

"I know, Mamu. You've told us a hundred times. Thank you, thank you, thank you. OK?"

"Keeping a filthy secret like that. You've got your father's blood, that's for certain."

"We all have our secrets, don't we, Mamu?" It was the only ammunition I had and I used it and it hit home.

"I thought better of you, Ben."

"So did I." I remembered what mother said to me the day she left. "People do a lot of things to survive and keeping secrets isn't the worst of them. You, of all people, have to know that."

I was blackmailing her and she knew it and was clearly disappointed. "I'm sorry I told you."

"What did you tell him?"

But before Mamu could answer Osceola came running into the kitchen.

"You goin' to have to wait to finish your talk. There's cars out there and a truck from a damn radio station. WNEX. News sure travels fast. 'Specially scandal kinda news." He walked through the kitchen, down the hall, and out the front door. We all followed him.

"Get off this property. Right now." He looked bigger than I had ever seen him as he stood on the porch facing the reporters who were clambering for a story.

"Who are you, nigger?" said the dark-haired Carl Thomas who had been the first to arrive.

"I'll tell you who I am. I'm the nigger who'll get the ax handle and lay it upside of your head if you don't get the hell away from here. That's who I am. Now, you go on back to the highway and don't you set one foot on this here private property or I will come down there and cut it off. You understand what I'm sayin' or do I have to make it any plainer?"

They all started firing questions at once, but they did start backing away from the house.

"Get those cars and that truck out of here." Mamu had stepped foreward. "We've got a business to run here."

"Ben," said Osceola, "get the sawhorses out of the gabarn and take the truck and drive them down to the highway and make a barrier. Ain't nothin' else goin' to stop them people. That probably won't even do it." He turned back to them. "Now, go on. Get out of here before I get the shotgun." As they started back toward their cars he pushed us into the house. "Estella, you better go down and tell Mr. Josh what's goin' on. I wouldn't put it past them reporters to come up the creek in a boat. And he don't know nothin' about what's happenin'."

Whatever quarrel we had with Mamu would have to wait. Estella headed for the creek and I got the sawhorses and drove down to the highway and herded the reporters off our property. They were all shouting questions at the same time, but all I could get was the occasional word or phrase: *sexual relationship, oddball, your own sister, knife, uppity nigger, murder.* I didn't say anything. They were crazed, in a frenzy, like the chickens scrambling for the first feed of the day. I got back in the truck and headed up Broadway.

Uncle Josh was in the kitchen reading the paper when I got to the house. Mamu must have been finishing with the goats or she was locked away in the sewing room. I didn't know which. Priddie was doing what she always did when she was upset: cooking.

"I wonder how often the McElways hid in the bushes and watched us? Do you think the *Register* actually paid them money for that picture or what?" Estella was reading over his shoulder.

"I can't blame Adela for being angry." Uncle Josh put the paper on the table.

"I know, but she wants you to pack up and go. It's our fault just as much as yours." She leaned over to examine the photo again. "Just look at me!"

"I can't blame her for wanting me to leave."

"You all just go out in the fields and get to work. Don't even come near here to pick up your baskets. Wait 'til the boys get here and let them do it for you. Things will settle down." I don't think Osceola believed what he was saying. "You know Miz Adela. She get her back up, but after awhile she calms down. You seen her do that a million times. Let me have a little time with her. Just get out of here so she don't see you now. This ain't the right time to be talkin' about things. Go out through the front door so she don't see you if she's comin' in from the goats."

"She's going to see me sooner or later," said Uncle Josh.

"Man, ain't you been listenin' to me. *Now* ain't the time. Sooner ain't nearly as good as later. So get the hell out of here."

Estella, Uncle Josh, and I hurried down the hall and out the front door and as we came out of the gate and crossed Broadway we could see a crowd of people behind the barrier I had made with the saw horses. When they saw us they started shouting, but we kept right on going without acknowledging them.

Chapter XIV

"Looks like it might rain," I said. The early morning sky was showing no sign of the sun. "Good. It will get those reporters all wet."

"It'll get us wet, too," said Estella. "I don't feel like standing out here in the rain until Mamu has cooled off enough for us to go home."

Uncle Josh was distracted. Weather was the least of his worries.

The boys weren't there yet and we had no baskets so we started half-heartedly picking the melons and piling them at the ends of the rows.

"If I were younger I'd go to Europe. Try and get in service in England or France. Don't know if they'd want me but I'd certainly try." Uncle Josh stopped picking and stared off into the distance. "But I'm too old. Even if I wasn't they wouldn't take me because I had TB." He looked down at his hands as though he was seeing them for the first time. "I don't think Adela will change her mind. I don't know why she should. I should have left here years ago. The problem is, I don't know where to go; I've never known. It's difficult for some people to make a move. I don't know what it is. I guess we settle in and just don't know how to go about changing things. We're frozen by our own indecision. I think that's what it is with me. I don't have any place I *want* to go."

I thought of all the pinpoints on his maps and all the places he wanted to go "some day."

"You don't have to go anyplace. Osceola's right, once things settle down and get back to normal Mamu will come around." Estella didn't like the idea of change. She always wanted everything to stay exactly the way it was.

"It's inevitable," said Uncle Josh. "We all know that. We've all known it ever since Gloria was murdered." He walked to the other end of the row and no one said anything for awhile. I wanted to say something reassuring, but I knew Uncle Josh was right. It was inevitable that he would leave. I think I knew it the day Mamu and I sat with him in the Laurelwood jail.

"Hey, Ben," Estella called after about fifteen minutes. "Do you think I look fat in that picture?" It was exactly what we needed to break the tension. I started laughing so hard I had trouble standing up and Uncle Josh just gave in and plopped down on the ground. "What's so funny?" asked Estella. "I do look fat, don't I?" That made us laugh even harder. Estella could never keep a straight face when anyone laughed and she started laughing with us, barely able to get any words out. "What the hell are we laughing at? I'm serious." The three of us ended up on the ground rolling around in the cantaloupes. It was as satisfying as the night of the shadow dancing.

When Stash and Janos arrived we were still carrying on and, of course, they joined in, not having any idea what we were laughing about.

"You OK?" asked Stash. "You want cigarette?"

"No, thank you. I'm OK."

"OK," said Janos, and took a cigarette.

"Lot of people on the highway." Stash lit a match and held it out to Janos before lighting his own.

"Yeah, a lot of people." I didn't want to have to explain what was going on. "Would you get us some baskets?"

"Yeah, sure. OK," said Janos and they started off for the gabarn.

"They show photo," said Stash over his shoulder.

"Oh, my God," shouted Estella, "They saw that fat picture of me! That naked, fat picture."

"Not fat," said Janos, more serious than I had ever seen him. "No, no. Not fat. Nice." And, for whatever reason, that seemed funnier than anything anyone had said before and we all started laughing again.

It was almost noon when we heard the ship's bell. Even though it was overcast I could feel the sunburn on my face. We had been working all morning with no hats. At first, when I heard the bell, I thought it was Osceola calling us in because Mamu had cooled off and changed her mind, but the ringing was frantic and insistent.

"Something's wrong," said Uncle Josh. "Come on. Hurry." We were several acres away and the three of us, along with Stash and Janos, ran toward the house as fast as we could. We had a signal for dinner or lunch. Three rings and no more. But this ringing was constant, demanding, and ominous.

The first people I saw were Mamu, Priddie, and Osceola standing on the porch so I knew they were all right. Priddie was standing near the bell so I assumed she had been ringing it. There was twice as big a crowd as there had been when I had put up the barrier earlier that morning. The radio truck was there and a long expensive-looking convertible was parked at the gate. Everyone seemed to be focusing on something on the lawn. When the reporters saw us they turned their attention our way and started firing questions and when the crowd parted, making way for us, I saw a middle-aged man, blond and aristocratic, standing between the gate and the porch. It was Claude Gardiner. I recognized him from pictures I had seen in the paper. Even though his hair was windblown and he was sweaty with his shirt hanging open, he looked like the fair-haired fantasy father Estella had talked about when we were children. He was definitely a man who looked as though he would be perfectly at home on a polo pony.

"I've called the police, Mr. Gardiner. They're on their way so you'd better get away from here." Mamu was using her most authoritarian voice, but it didn't sound very convincing. "All of you people, get away from here. This is private property."

"Mr. Josh, you stay back," warned Osceola. "This man ain't in his right mind."

Gardiner turned to see who Osceola was talking to and saw Uncle Josh. The crowd quieted down, waiting to see what would happen next.

"So you're the one who was screwing my wife. I wanted to get a look at you." His eyes were wide and wild. "What in hell did she ever see in trash like you."

"You shut up," said Estella and started toward him but Stash, who was standing right behind her, grabbed hold of her arms and stopped her.

"Estella, you stay out of this." Osceola stepped down off the porch. "Listen Mr. Gardiner, ain't none of this goin' to do anybody any good. You'd be better off if you just get the hell out of here before any trouble starts."

"She was my wife, goddamn it!" he screamed. "My wife!"

"I loved her," said Uncle Josh.

"Then you loved a whore." He started crying. They weren't tears of sadness; they were clearly tears of rage.

I could hear the police siren as the car came racing down Broadway. It pulled to a stop, brakes squeaking, sending up a cloud of dust, and Sheriff Anderson and Adam got out.

"What's going on here?" said the sheriff as he pushed through the crowd.

Claude Gardiner ignored him. "She was a whore and she deserved to die. My son hates me because of her. Even if she wasn't a whore, she deserved to die. But that other man didn't. He was innocent. I killed an innocent man because of you." The reporters started talking at once as cameras clicked. He had just announced to the police and the world that he had killed his wife and Marius Dorfman.

"Shut up," he yelled at the reporters. "Shut up, goddamn it!" He had nothing to lose now. When they were quiet he said, "Write this down." He took a step in the direction of Uncle Josh. "He killed an innocent man, too. He killed him just as much as I did. It was all his fault."

"You're right," said Uncle Josh. "I killed him. I killed him because I wasn't there that night. It should have been me."

Later, Adam said that Gardiner's next move was a suicide attempt. From under his shirt he pulled a hunting knife and raised it threateningly to Uncle Josh. At first there was a shocked silence, but then people stared screaming. He made no move to attack Uncle Josh, he just stood with the knife in his hand. Adam and the sheriff grabbed their guns, but before they could aim, Osceola and the boys and I jumped Claude Gardiner and wrestled him to the ground. He didn't resist, but Osceola and Stash were hurt in the scuffle and there was blood all over the place. At first we all thought we had been cut.

I don't remember the next few minutes very clearly. There was a lot of shouting and picture-taking and Adam and the sheriff handcuffed Gardiner and put him in the back of the police car and drove off. There was absolutely no resistance on his part. I do remember Adam touching Estella's arm and saying something to her just before they left. Most of the reporters ran down Broadway to the highway to get their cars. A few tried to talk to us, but a ferocious Osceola, holding his bleeding arm, threatened them, and finally scared them off. We all went into the house, shaken, exhausted, but exhilarated at the same time. Priddie decided no one needed stitches, so she and Estella dressed the wounds.

"Just about a half a inch and he would have cut your jugular vein and you would a bled to death," said Priddie as she applied her special herb salve to Stash's neck. Estella handed her the bandage. "Don't you go gettin' this bandage dirty. I'll change it for you tomorrow. Then, as soon as it starts closin' up we let the fresh air do the rest of the work."

"You boys go on home," said Osceola once he was taken care of. "Ain't goin' to be no work done around here today."

Stash looked at Mamu. "Yes?"

She didn't answer. Instead, she turned and looked out the window. Uncle Josh was standing by the mud porch door, watching her.

"Go on," said Osceola to the boys. "Get the hell out of here. And if your neck don't feel right tomorrow, don't come in. Ain't goin' to be a normal day anyway and it ain't goin' to do your neck any good bendin' over."

"That's right," said Priddie, "bendin' could open it up and then where are you?"

"Besides," Osceola rolled down his sleeve, "them people from the papers will be all over the damn place."

"OK, OK." The two of them went out through the mud porch and I could hear Janos laughing as they crossed the yard.

We were all in shock and for awhile no one said anything.

"Well, it's all over." Osceola took out his handkerchief and mopped his brow. "But it's only the beginnin' for them reporters. We're all goin' to be world-famous. Can you beat that? Hell, we'll be gettin' orders for vegetables all the way from China and Timbuktu. Like I always say, it pays to advertise." He laughed, but no one joined in. The phone rang. "You see, it's startin' already."

I went down the hall and answered. It was Adam wanting to know if Stash and Osceola were all right.

"Yeah, they're fine. Priddie took care of them."

"They don't have to see a doctor?"

"No, they're going to be OK. Just flesh wounds. What's happening with Mr. Gardiner?"

"He's just sitting in the cell like he's in a trance or something. We're waiting for them to come and take him to the county jail. I look at him and I think, there's a man who had everything a person could ever want. And he's sitting there waiting to go to the county jail. Things just plain don't make sense sometime. I guess he's as relieved as the rest of us that we know the truth. He's kind of sad looking . . . that's not the right thing to say about a murderer, is it, if you know what I mean."

"Yeah, I do."

"Can I talk to Estella?"

"Just a minute." I put down the phone and went to the kitchen. "Estella, it's for you."

"Me? A reporter?"

"No, it's Adam." Things had changed. Only the day before I wouldn't have been able to say Adam wanted to talk to Estella. I would have been afraid of what Mamu's reaction would be but, after all that had happened, it didn't make any difference. "When you finish talking to him leave the receiver off the hook."

"I will." She went to the phone.

There was another awkward silence. I don't know if everyone was lost in their thoughts or, like me, they were wondering what was going to happen between Uncle Josh and Mamu. He made the first move.

"Adela. . . ." he took a step toward her and she turned to him.

"Leave here." She said it calmly, knowing full well that he was expecting her to say it.

"I was going to say I was leaving." There was resignation in his voice. "I'm sorry about everything."

"Your apologies don't mean a thing to me. Just leave."

Priddie and Osceola said nothing. I suppose, like Uncle Josh, they knew it was inevitable and they were resigned. I knew it, too, but I hated this blind acceptance as much as I hated life going on when the world was crumbling all around me.

"If Uncle Josh leaves, I'm leaving, too."

"Ben. . . ." he said.

"I mean it, Mamu. I'll go. I swear I will." She looked at me and almost smiled. "If Uncle Josh goes, I'll go with him. All you have to do is ask him to stay. He didn't do anything so terrible. Ask him to stay. Please. One little word. Stay."

"No."

"Why does he have to leave?"

"Because I don't want him here. I don't trust him."

"Ben, it's all right," said Uncle Josh.

"Then I'm going."

"That's up to you." She went down the hall and up the stairs to her room. Priddie had her apron up to her mouth and Osceola just shook his head.

"This isn't right, Ben." Uncle Josh turned to Osceola but he didn't say anything.

"What the hell have I done?" He went out through the mud porch.

"I don't have a suitcase." I couldn't think of anything else to say.

"You really want to go, Ben? It ain't too late to change your mind." Priddie went to Osceola and stood next to him. I could hear Estella laughing and talking to Adam.

Did I really want to go? I was frightened, but I felt it was too late to change my mind. I told Mamu I was leaving and there was no turning back. "Yes. I do."

"Then I'll bring you a suitcase tomorrow. I'm not rushin' you. It's up to you to go whenever you want. But a man has to have a suitcase just in case he gets it under his skin to move on." It was the way he talked to me when I was a child . . . a man has to do this and a man has to do that. It was the easiest way to get me to do things. "You remind me, Priddie. That suitcase my daddy got for me when I came north. You know the one I'm talkin' about."

"I know." Priddie came to me and hugged me. Human contact was a rare commodity and I never needed it more than I did then. The touch of her warm little body was almost too much to bear.

"I'm going to go and clean up." I still had blood all over me. "I don't know if it's your blood or Stash's."

"It don't much matter." Osceola smiled. "As long as it ain't your own blood."

I went down the hall and as I passed Estella she covered the mouthpiece.

"You OK?"

"Fine."

"What's going on?"

"I'll tell you later."

"OK." She went back to the phone. "Hello . . . no, I was talking to Ben. So, what were you saying?"

Mamu's door was shut and I listened for a moment, but didn't hear anything. I went into the bathroom, ran a tub, and when I settled into the soothing hot water, the realization hit me. There was no way out of it. I was leaving Broadway Acres.

The rest of the day was as isolating for everyone as solitary confinement. Osceola parked the truck at the end of Broadway, just off the highway, blocking the entrance so the reporters couldn't get to us. By then, our names were being wired all over the world. It was inconceivable. I spent the afternoon in my room thinking about leaving. Wondering where we'd go. It took me no time at all to fold my clothes so they'd be ready when Osceola brought the suitcase because I really didn't have that many. I went through my treasure chest and decided it was time to throw everything away. The only things I was going to take, aside from my clothes, were my travelers' guide to Venice and the deck of cards with the missing king of hearts. I have no idea why I took the deck, but I still have it.

The sun never came out, but it didn't rain and the afternoon was cool and lazy. I lay on my bed thinking about the events of the day, sometimes not quite sure any of it had really happened.

Estella came to my room early evening. Priddie had told her I was planning on leaving.

"Are you really going?"

"Yeah. I have to."

"I knew this was going to happen. I don't want you to go."

"Come with us."

"Where are you going?"

"I don't know. I haven't talked to Uncle Josh yet."

"How can I go? I just can't pick up and leave."

"That's what I'm going to do. Come on. You were always the adventurous one. At least you said you were."

"And leave Mamu here alone? There'll be no one in the house at night but her. I can't do that." She had spent an hour on the phone with Adam. She wasn't about to run off with Uncle Josh and me. Everything had changed for her.

"Yeah, you're right. Somebody has to stay here. Have you talked to her?"

"No. She hasn't come out of her room. I bet she won't come out until tomorrow when it's time for the goats." She went to the dresser and looked at the clothes neatly piled on top. "When do you think you'll leave?"

"I don't know. Soon, I guess. You want to walk down to the shack with me and talk to Uncle Josh?"

"I promised Priddie I'd help her with supper."

We went downstairs together and I went on out through the mud porch.

"Where you off to?" asked Priddie.

"To the shack."

"You tell Mr. Josh we'll have supper in about an hour." Then I heard her say to Estella, "I don't expect either one of them is too hungry. Lord, what is happenin' to this family?"

He wasn't in the shack. Everything was as tidy as always, but his clothes were missing and when I looked around some of the recordings were gone. I had a sick, empty feeling in my stomach. I went out on the dock and discovered he had taken the rowboat. There was no mystery about his going. He left without telling me so I wouldn't have to leave. He must have thought it was the right thing to do. I knew that, but I felt abandoned, left to make a decision I wasn't at all sure I could make. I also knew that if I walked along the creek I'd find the boat. It was the same overgrown and treacherous path I had taken the night I walked along in my nakedness, stumbling and cutting myself on the brambles. The rowboat was tied to a sapling near the bridge, just before the lake. He must have tied it there and walked up to the bridge to hitch a ride to wherever he was going. There were pieces of a broken record in the bottom of the boat. *Liszt's Second Hungarian Rhapsody*, one of our favorites. I got in the boat and rowed it back to the dock and when I got there Estella was waiting for me.

"I wondered what the hell happened to you. Supper's ready. Where's Uncle Josh?"

"Gone."

"He left without you? How could he do that? Did he tell you to say goodbye for him?"

"I didn't see him. I found the rowboat by the bridge." I tied it to the piling.

"Oh, God, you don't think he killed himself, do you?"

"No, he didn't kill himself. He took his clothes and some records. You don't take clothes and records when you're going to kill yourself, do you?" I walked up the path to the dock. "He left me alone. Damn him!"

"Now you don't have to go."

"Of course, I have to go. Jesus, you don't understand anything."

"Don't holler at me."

"It's so easy for you, isn't it?" Even as I was yelling at her I knew my anger had nothing to do with Estella. "You don't have to go any-place or do anything. It's all going to work out for you. You've got Adam and you've got your whole future all planned. What do you have to worry about?"

"God! All I said was you don't have to go."

"I do. Don't you know that! I have to go. That's all there is to it." She followed me into the shack.

"So what if Mamu wins again?"

"Just shut up, Estella. Do me a big favor and shut up." I sat on the edge of the bed and we didn't say anything for a few moments.

"He didn't take any of his books." Estella's voice was small and apologetic. "There doesn't seem to be a single book missing. Maybe I should pack them in boxes and wait until he tells us what to do with them. He'll want his books, won't he?"

"I guess."

"Maybe he'll come back in a couple of weeks."

"I don't think so."

"And all his extra maps are here."

"Let me see those." She handed me the large stack of maps. "I wonder if he has an extra one of New Jersey?"

I found a very colorful and fanciful map of the world and almost at the bottom of the pile, a Rand McNally map of New Jersey. "New Jersey, *The Garden State*, was one of the original thirteen colonies . . ." was the beginning of the information in a box on the cover. I read it to Estella and she came and sat next to me on the bed.

"I'm sorry, Ben." She started crying. I put my arms around her.

"No, I'm sorry. I'm just mad that he left me here and I took it out on you. I don't know what to do, but I know I have to go." We were holding each other, rocking back and forth. "Maybe I'm one of those people Uncle Josh was talking about. One of the people who doesn't know how to make a move, frozen by their own indecision. Remember when he said that this morning? Jesus, was that only this morning?"

"I'm going to miss you."

"It won't be forever."

"No, it won't." She kissed me on the lips, but this time it was different. The only other time we had kissed she had wanted Adam and didn't know if she'd ever have him. Rightly so, I was a momentary substitute. Things had changed. "Let's go. Priddie will be mad at us for being so late."

When we got back to the house we told Priddie and Osceola that Uncle Josh had left.

"Well," said Osceola, "ain't the press goin' to have a field day with this. Can't get much better than a ex-lover and suspected murderer suddenly disappearin'. Juicy stuff, ain't it."

"I can't believe he'd just up and leave without sayin' anything." I think Priddie was hurt that he didn't say goodbye to her. "It don't seem right."

"Wasn't nothin' else he could do," said Osceola. "it don't surprise me one little bit. No sir, not one little bit."

The next morning when I came downstairs, Priddie and Osceola were having their coffee. As promised, they brought the suitcase. It was old, but in very good condition, brown leather and heavy as lead even when it was empty.

"Where's Mamu?"

"Out with the goats. She finished with the milking and put it in the springhouse, but she went back out. She wasn't what you'd call talkative this morning. And Estella came down and got a glass of orange juice and went back up to her room."

"Everythin' is wrong," said Priddie. "That's the only word for it. Wrong. That's a terrible feelin'."

"You don't have to pack up and go, you know, but now you got your own suitcase if you want to." Osceola picked up the paper and pretended to be reading it.

"I'm going this morning. Will you take me to Laurelwood? I want to get the train."

"Where you goin' to go?" asked Priddie. "Now that Mr. Josh is gone, you on your own. Just where are you goin'?"

I had studied the maps most of the night. The map of New Jersey almost overpowered me as much as the map of the world. The map of the world had Jakarta, Katmandu, Zaragoza, and Maracaibo, and New Jersey had Weehawken, Parsippany, Wanamassa, and Piscataway. They all sounded equally mysterious and seductive, but as far away and unattainable as the moon. The only world I had known had the kitchen as its epicenter and anything and everything that shook it up emanated from there. I needed a place with a name as simple and solid as Millersburg, but at the same time a city that had all I was certain a city had to offer. I thought of going to New

York, but the circus experience had never left me—I always pictured it as threatening and grotesque, and it was in another state. I passed on Philadelphia for the same reason. It was as though I thought I'd need a passport and lessons in another language if I left New Jersey.

"I still don't know, but I want to get to the train station. I'll make up my mind then. I have a list of places."

"You can't just go. . . ." Priddie started to protest but Osceola stopped her.

"That's enough. He knows what he wants to do so you just stay out of it."

"All right, all right. Give him the money," she said.

"I have some money. I don't need any."

"How much?" asked Osceola.

"About a hundred dollars." It seemed like a fortune to me.

"Well, that's a good start but, it ain't enough. Here." He handed me a wad of bills. "There's five hundred dollars there. That'll keep you goin' for awhile. 'Til you get a job. We brought it just in case you decided to go."

"I can't take your money. . . ."

"You ain't takin' our money. It's a loan. When you're on your feet, you pay us back."

"It's only money, Ben, so there's the end to that," said Priddie. She turned away and went back to setting the table. "Well, if you're leavin' you have to eat a good breakfast. And don't you say you don't want any 'cause I ain't listenin' to that."

"What about your schoolin'? Did you think about that?" Osceola fixed me with his eyes. "It's about time to go back to school. This is your last year and you're out of high school. Schoolin's mighty important."

I had thought about school and decided if I put off leaving I might never go. And I didn't know how I'd get through another year with Mamu. "I'll finish later. I can always go back."

"There's no talkin' you out of it, is there?" She took my hand and held it to her breast. "You're really leavin' us, ain't you?" She kissed the back of my hand. "Yeah, you are. Then, go on up and pack the suitcase if you want Osceola to drive you to the station."

I knocked on Estella's door on the way to my room.

"Come on in."

"Are you coming down for breakfast?"

"No. I don't feel like it. I'm going to stay up here until you leave. Do you mind?"

She was sitting on the side of her bed, still in her nightgown with her thick black hair, so dark it shone blue, hanging over her shoulders. She was beautiful.

"You'll let me know where you are, won't you?"

"When I know where I am, you'll know where I am."

"OK."

"You think I'm running out on you?"

"No. But even if I did, it doesn't matter. I know you have to go. You take good care."

She made no move to come to me so I stayed in the doorway. "See ya."

"Yeah. See ya."

I closed her door, went up, and packed my things. I put the maps on top of the clothes, so they'd be available for quick reference.

The breakfast Priddie made for me was enough for a platoon of men. The three of us ate in silence, Even Osceola, who was rarely at a loss for words, couldn't think of anything to say.

"I'm going to say goodbye to Mamu," I said when I had finished eating as much as I could.

"I'll start up the truck."

I went to the gabarn to look for her. She was standing in the shadows petting the goats. She hadn't wrapped her braid into the bun. It was hanging over her right shoulder and made her look strangely vulnerable.

"I'm leaving, Mamu." She didn't answer. "I'm sorry. . . ."

"Yes. Everyone is sorry and it doesn't change a thing. Are you going to stay with your mother and father? I understand Joshua has run out on you."

"I wouldn't call it running out on me. I think he left because he didn't want me to feel I had to go."

"He left because he didn't want you tagging along."

"That's not true."

"You'd be a responsibility. He'd walk through the fires of hell to get away from any kind of responsibility. Why can't you see that?"

"I don't believe it."

"How long are you going to go on defending him? Nothing sadder than misplaced loyalty. It's like a disease."

"Well, it's my disease, not yours. And I'm not staying with mother. I'm not sure where I'm going."

"Quite an adventurer, aren't you?" She picked a piece of hay out of Masha's coat. "What about school? You were so anxious to finish school."

"I will . . . someday."

"I see. Then you've got this all planned."

"No, I don't. Like I said, I don't even know where I'm going. Mamu. . . ." I wanted to say that maybe one day everything would be all right between us, that I'd go away for a little while and then come back but she interrupted.

"You'd better go."

"Yes. Well . . . goodbye." I started to walk away, but stopped and turned to her. "One thing, I'll never tell anyone what you told me. You know, about grandfather."

She looked at me for a moment. "I doubt that." She turned and walked deep into the shadows of the gabarn and I went back to the house.

My suitcase was in the truck and Priddie was waiting to say goodbye. She had packed me a lunch.

"Hurry up, boy. Let's get on the road before the reporters show up and we get stuck in the house."

"We goin' to miss you, Ben." She hugged me and whispered in my ear. "We love you. You know that, don't you?"

"Yes. And I love you." I had never said those words before. It was easier than I thought it would be.

"Let's get goin'. Who's goin' to drive? You or me?" asked Osceola.

"You drive." I climbed into the truck.

"That's the first time I ever heard you say that. Lord amighty! You finally know which one of us is the best driver. You ain't as dumb as you look."

"You let us know where you are, you hear," said Priddie. "We goin' to miss you somethin' terrible."

Osceola pulled away. As we went down Broadway the guineas and geese started squabbling and Sinclair raced back and forth in his paddock as though he was anxious to go along, too. I looked up and saw Estella standing in the hall window. She waved just before we passed under the maple tree. We drove along the road mother had taken everyday for all those years and I thought about the day I followed her in the truck. Everything seemed to have happened so long ago, but it was only a matter of weeks.

"Will you tell mother. . . ."

"You want to drop by and see her? It ain't like we're tryin' to keep to a schedule."

"No." I didn't want to see Devlin. "That's OK."

"I put your mother and father's phone number and address in your suitcase. You know ours. It ain't goin' to hurt you to write to them."

We drove through the center of Laurelwood past the courthouse where Uncle Josh had been held and the Rexall drug store where I had the lonely lunch and turned left on Emmerson. "Just drop me off in front of the station," I said. "You don't have to come in."

"I want to come in. I want to see you get on that train."

"Well, I don't want you to. Please."

"You sure?"

"Yeah. I'm sure."

"Whatever you say."

"I know with Uncle Josh and me leaving you're going to be short-handed . . ."

"Don't you worry about us. Winter will be comin' on soon. Besides, you got to do what you got to do. Get out there and find out what it's all about. Then maybe you come home. Don't worry one little bit about us. We'll manage. Them boys ain't as bad as your grandmother makes them out to be. Janos works pretty good, but that laughin' drives me crazy. But Stash, well he's a good man and a damn hard worker."

"Yeah, he is."

"You scared?"

"I've never been so scared in my life."

"Good. At least that shows you got some sense. Remember, you need anythin' . . . anythin' at all you just call. More important than that, if you change your mind, you come on home. You hear me? You just come on home."

"I will."

We pulled up in front of the train station and I got out.

"Don't forget your suitcase," he said. "And Priddie packed you enough food to feed Cox's army." He put out his hand and I took it. That great, strong black hand with the white palm that had picked me up more times than I could remember. We didn't shake hands. We just held on to each other for a moment.

"Thanks for everything."

"We goin' to miss you, boy." He pulled his hand away and I could see his eyes glistening. "Don't you take any wooden nickels, now. You hear?" He put the truck in gear and drove away and I stood there for the longest time, part of me hoping he'd come back and tell me I didn't have to go.

I went into the station, opened my suitcase, and took out my map and my list of possible destinations. The whole place smelled of stale cigarettes. Scattered around on the walls of the waiting room were some sooty framed pictures of places it was impossible to get to from the Laurelwood train station: the Alps, Hong Kong harbor, and the Pyramids. There were about twenty people sitting uncomfortably on the hard wooden benches, reading papers or books or simply daydreaming. An elderly couple with no luggage so I assumed they were on a day trip, a very old lady holding tight to a suitcase with a rope tied around to hold it together, a woman with a child asleep in her lap, and several businessmen. They automatically looked at everyone coming into the waiting room, but didn't really see them. One quick glance and they retreated to that place in the mind the occupies strangers in a crowd. My list was as baffling in the station as it had been the night before in my bedroom. They were still merely names of towns and it didn't matter which one I chose because I knew next to nothing about any of them. I don't know how long I was there before I finally put the map and list back in the suitcase and went to the window and bought a one-way ticket.